THE CIRCLE OPENS

MAGIC STEPS

BOOK ONE OF
THE CIRCLE OPENS
QUARTET

● TAMORA PIERCE ●

SCHOLASTIC PRESS

33415

Library of Congress Cataloging-in-Publication Data
Pierce, Tamora.
Magic steps / by Tamora Pierce
p. cm. — (The circle opens)
Summary: When drawn into the investigation of murders perpetrated
on a powerful family in Summersea, Sandry and her student Pasco
undertake the dangerous mission of entrapping the invisible killers.

ISBN 0-590-39588-2

[1. Magic Fiction. 2. Fantasy.]
I. Title. II. Series: Pierce, Tamora. Circle opens.
PZ7.P61464Mag 2000
[Fic]—DC21 99-31943 CIP
10 9 8 7 6 5 4 3 2   0/0 01 02 03 04 05

Printed in the U.S.A.
First edition, March 2000
Book design by Elizabeth Parisi

To Anne.
This book—this quartet—would probably never have been written if not for you.

Lady Sandrilene fa Toren opened the door to her room and stepped into the dark corridor. She was dressed for riding in broad-legged breeches, tunic, and blouse, and in one hand she carried her riding boots. In the other she held a round blob of crystal threaded with dark lines. It shone brightly and steadily against the gloom. The hour was early enough that most of the servants were still abed, and the torches set to burn in the halls the night before had guttered out.

Holding up her stone to light the way, Sandry padded down the corridor in stockinged feet. It was because of the servants that she made so little noise. In six weeks' residence at the castle, she had learned that most of them were light sleepers. No amount of persuasion that she could look after herself quite nicely, thank you, was enough to send them back to bed. They would rise at dawn anyway — why cause them to lose as much as an hour of rest when they worked so hard?

As she passed a high table, she noted that the candlesticks atop it stood on a rumpled length of embroidered cloth. She reached out a hand. The cloth shifted until it lay flat and neat on the wood. A silk rug knocked askew slid in her wake until it lay straight again.

She plopped herself onto the top stair and tugged on her riding boots, then frowned. A light showed under the door of a ground-floor room that opened onto the entrance hall.

Uncle, she thought, vexed. And what odds that he hasn't been up since four? With a sigh, she trotted downstairs and entered the room, a small library. There sat her great-uncle in a wing-backed chair. He was reading a sheaf of papers by the light shed by a crystal globe. The globe was larger than Sandry's, perfectly round and without flaws, its light as steady as the sun's.

Inspecting his stark white shirt, black tunic, and breeches, Sandry decided she would have to do something about the duke's clothes. He liked to dress plainly, but there was no law that said he had to wear blacks, browns, and dark blues without any bright colors. A crimson tunic might warm his skin tone, and a touch of gold embroidery at his collar would add sparkle to his eyes. Until he was fully recovered from his recent heart attack, he would need such aids to keep his people from thinking he might still die.

And it won't hurt to stitch in signs for health and

strength, either, she thought, fingers already itching to pick up needle and thread. "Uncle," she announced crisply, "just because the healers say you may ride again does *not* mean you are ready to take up your old work schedule as well."

Duke Vedris IV, ruler of Emelan, looked up at his favorite great-niece and smiled. The smile warmed a face that was still haggard, though he looked better to Sandry's critical eye than he had even a week ago. He needs to smile more, she thought. Without affection or amusement to light his eyes, he was a rather forbidding middle-aged man with fleshy features, deepset brown eyes, and an eagle's nose. With some warm feeling in his face, he looked both serious and kind, the sort of man it was easy to trust and depend on.

"This isn't work," the duke told her as he lifted the sheaf of parchments. "I'm just reviewing what's been done on the repairs to the harbor wall."

Sandry walked over to him, kissed his forehead, and drew the papers from his fingers. "The harbormaster is an expert on this sort of thing. You told me so yourself. And you know what Dedicate Comfrey said — why pay these people if you have to watch them all the time?"

"I'm not watching. I'm keeping myself up-to-date." The duke carefully got to his feet. Sandry did not try to help. Too many people did that, and it upset him far more than did the loss of his former strength. "You and

Dedicate Comfrey should understand that sooner or later I must begin to oversee my realm once more."

"I can't wait until you do," she told him pertly. "You're getting awfully hard to handle."

He laughed at that. "I'm going to miss you when you return to Winding Circle," he remarked, going to the door. "You're the only one who is completely frank with me."

As he left the room, Sandry put the papers she had taken on his desk. For a moment she stayed there, staring blindly at the curtained windows. As much as she wanted to return home, she worried about him. Over and over she had heard tales of the way he lived, skipping meals and going without sleep to complete some piece of work. His household was in awe of Duke Vedris, and feared to balk him. Without her there to keep an eye on things, he would probably return to his old bad habits.

She didn't like that thought. Emelan's best healer-mages had warned her that while they had done all they could to strengthen his heart and veins, he was vulnerable to another attack. A second one might well kill him; a third definitely would.

He managed without a meddling fourteen-year-old for years, one voice said in her mind.

He was younger then, argued a second.

Sandry growled with impatience — she had been listening to this internal argument for weeks — and flung her hands wide. The heavy draperies on the windows flew apart to bare expensive glass panes. The thick gold ropes that held the curtains open wrapped around the lengths of cloth and tied themselves, then let their tasseled ends dangle neatly.

Getting her worries under control, Sandry followed her uncle to the main door. It was open already, offering a view of the stone courtyard, a score of burning torches, and a squad of the Duke's Guardsmen and their horses.

Duke Vedris waited for her to reach him and offered his arm. His dark eyes searched her face intently. "Did I say anything to distress you, my dear?" he asked quietly.

Sandry shook her head and made herself smile. "The only thing that distresses me is the thought that you got up early this morning to read papers," she informed him. "You're supposed to rest, Uncle!" As they walked down the stair to their mounts, she thought, And what will Lark say if I stay with him?

"Pasco. Pasco, wake up."

He rolled over and moaned.

A hand grabbed his shoulder. "Pasco, you chuff', getting up was *your* idea. Now do it — I want to go to bed."

Pasco Acalon sat up, blinking. His sister Halmaedy knelt by the bed, her dark eyes amused. She was still dressed for the watch that had just ended, the brown leather of her jerkin stark against her dark blue shirt and breeches.

Pasco rubbed his face, ordering his traitorous body to move. "'S a *disgusting* hour to be about," he grumbled.

"No arguments here. What's the deal, anyway?"

Pasco swung his legs out from under the blanket and leaned against his oldest sister. Their long, amber-skinned faces labeled them as kin: the same winged black brows over ebony-colored eyes, noses a little too short, and straight mouths a little too wide. At twelve Pasco was just starting to get his growth, his thin body coltish as he wrestled with arms and legs that tended to go every which way.

"A friend wants a favor," the boy mumbled as he pulled on his garments, tying the string that held up his breeches as tight as he could manage. His shirt required no buttoning, which was why he'd picked it out last night. The less he had to do before he was properly awake, the better.

"What kind of favor?" Halmaedy demanded, suspicious. "This isn't off the straight, is it? Because —"

Pasco ruffled her hair — glossy black, cropped short on the sides and left to grow long on top, just like his. "You're home now," he reminded her. "No need for harrier work here." Harrier was street slang for a Provost's Guard. "An Acalon off the straight?" he went on, his voice strangled as he bent over to don his shoes. "The very skies would cry at it. Go to bed, Halmy. Try to dream of something beside arresting drunks and house-breakers."

She punched at her brother halfheartedly; he ducked under her fist, blew a kiss at her, and left his room. He didn't bother to sneak by the garret room where the maids were — they had proved able to snore through hurricanes and his mother's first shout for them to get out of bed — but was quieter going down the stairs. He went noiselessly past his sisters' rooms and ghosted past the floor where his parents slept. Mama was the one to step quietly for. Once his father fell asleep, only his snoring proved he was not dead. Mama had the fox-ears, asleep and awake.

Down to the ground floor, a quick nip into the kitchen for some bread, then a five-minute jog to the docks. Osabo Netmender was in his boat at Godsluck Wharf. Once Pasco was aboard, Osa put his back into the oars, hauling the boat clear of the commercial docks and guiding it east, along Summersea's shoreline.

"I can't believe you're out of bed," Osa told his friend.

"Halmy woke me after her watch," said Pasco, yawning. "Look, this isn't some joke, is it? Your dad really thinks I can bring luck to his ship?"

"It's no joke," replied Osa, rowing with practiced ease. "Not when he's promised to pay you a silver crescent. Pa never jokes about money. And it's the whole fleet, not just our boat."

Pasco shook his head. A silver crescent was too much money for any kind of jest. "I just don't understand," he muttered, stretching.

"Look, you danced for luck on the entrance examinations, and the temple took me to be a student there," Osa said reasonably. "You danced luck for Adesina, and her baby popped out slick as seaweed —"

"Stop it," ordered Pasco. "That baby would've come easy without anyone's help. There was a temple midwife with her the whole time."

"And what was a temple birth-mage doing walking by the fishing village at just the right moment?" argued Osa.

"I'll bet you a copper crescent my dancing for fish don't do a whisper of good," Pasco told his friend.

The other boy winced. "That's too much like ill-wishing," he said, "We need the fish, Pasco. We need 'em bad."

"I'm not ill-wishing," retorted Pasco, offering some of his bread. Osa took a piece. "I just never heard of a dance that brought fish into nets before."

"Gran says it's an old one," Osa said doggedly. "She's gonna teach it to you. There's a song to go with it and everything. You'll see."

Pasco shrugged, and ate his breakfast in silence.

TAMORA PIERCE

* * *

Despite the early hour, there were people about as the duke's party rode east on Harbor Street, past Summersea's famed wharves. How the word got ahead of them Sandry couldn't guess, but some of those who started their day before dawn gathered along the way to greet their duke. Sailors, washerwomen, draymen — their eager looks and open smiles showed how glad they were to see Duke Vedris up and about. Sandry had meant to turn back once they reached Long Wharf but, looking ahead, she could see more of the locals emerging from ships and warehouses to get a look at him.

Cat dirt, she thought, vexed. She didn't want him to do too much today, after four weeks in bed and two weeks confined to his palace. At the same time she knew his people had been frightened by his illness. They wanted to reassure themselves that he was all right. One of the things he'd mentioned so often in their talks since his heart attack was the need to keep a realm stable. People who thought it might all go to pieces at any minute tended to do foolish things, like pull their money from the banks, which would make them collapse, or plot to set a new, stronger ruler on the throne.

Sandry watched her uncle as he patted the hand of a stout woman who had been coiling rope on one of the wharves. In this light — a combination of lanterns,

9

torches, and a pale sky — it was hard to tell if he was tired yet. He seemed more energetic than he'd been at Duke's Citadel, but it could be an act.

She looked at the grizzled sergeant in charge of their troop of guards. Last night she had made a point of finding the man and having a long chat with him about today's ride. Now he nudged his mount over until they were side by side.

"He takes strength from them, milady," the sergeant told her quietly. "Same as they do from him. I say let 'im go on a bit."

Sandry thought over what he'd said. At last she replied, "I suppose there's no harm in going on. If it looks like he's tiring, though, we turn back."

The sergeant bowed and returned to his soldiers. The word was passed among them in scant whispers.

Sandry looked at the duke to find his eyes were on her. He raised his eyebrows, and Sandry began to giggle. Trust her uncle to guess what the conversation had been about!

On they rode, past Jansar Wharf and Sharyn Wharf. The duke seemed to be enjoying himself, until he looked up and saw a fat, turbaned man emerged from the doorway of a large, gray stone building. Over the lintel was the sign ROKAT HOUSE: MYRRH AND FINE SPICES in large, gilded letters. People moved out of the man's way. Some of them, slower than their neighbors, were urged to do so by one of the three bruisers who came with him, two men and a woman with arms like a blacksmith's.

Sandry could feel the moment the Duke's Guards noticed the rough types. She heard a creak of leather, a hushed clink of metal, and four of the squad urged their horses up on either side of Vedris. Two more rode next to Sandry: they had been assigned to her since her arrival at Duke's Citadel and had proved themselves to be quiet, quick shadows.

The duke raised a hand, and all of his group halted. The fat man came forward until he stood just ten feet away and bowed low, his palms pressed together before his face. His guards also bowed, though not so low that they lost sight of the duke's protectors.

"Good morning, Rokat," the duke said. His velvety voice had gone very cold.

"May the gods be praised, your grace!" said the fat man, straightening. "It is a grand thing, to see you among your people once more." Now that he was closer, Sandry could tell that he wore a jeweled pin in the neat green folds of his turban and that his clothes were made of the finest silk that money could buy. His plump hands glittered with rings, all gold and most sporting a gem. After living with a smith for four years, she could also tell the bodyguards' weapons were very good and bore signs of earnest use.

"It was unnecessary for you to leave your counting-house to give me these felicitations," the duke replied.

"But I had to express my joy," replied the man — Rokat, the duke had called him — as he bowed again. "Seeing you is reassurance that the peace and law of your realm will continue to be kept. Seeing you, those of us who shelter in this safe harbor know we need fear no withdrawal of protection."

"Is there any reason I would consider such a withdrawal?" inquired the duke, leaning on his saddle horn.

"Never, your grace," said the fat man. "Never. I hope to see you again soon. Congratulations on your restored health!"

He waddled back to Rokat House. One of his guards sprang forward to open the door; the other two closed in swiftly behind him, guarding his back. Only when the quartet had gone inside Rokat House did Sandry feel a relaxing among the soldiers around her.

"Let us continue," Duke Vedris announced. The guards who had flanked her and her uncle fell back into their normal formation, and they resumed their ride.

"Who was that?" Sandry wanted to know.

"Rokat," the sergeant growled behind them, and spat.

"Jamar Rokat," Vedris said, nodding to a maid who was opening a set of shutters nearby. "Head of Rokat

House here in Summersea. They hold the monopoly on the myrrh trade and import other items. They behave within my borders, but elsewhere they are little better than pirates. They know I will have none of the killing and thievery they use as common coin, and they dare not lose permission to enter our harbor."

"Is this Jamar as bad as the rest of his family?" Sandry wanted to know. There had been something about the fat man's brown eyes, a nervousness, that made her curious.

The duke rubbed his shaved head. "When Jamar Rokat was but twenty years old and living in Janaal, he was courting a young girl of great beauty and fortune. Somehow the word got out that the girl's father was considering another man, one who had offered more gold in the marriage settlement. Jamar entered his rival's house and with a silk cord strangled the man, his father, and his grandfather. He desired to make the point that competing with any Rokat was a fatal exercise."

Sandry shuddered.

The duke leaned over to pat her knee. "Fortunately, my dear, you need have nothing to do with any of Rokat's tribe. For that, I am thankful."

Pasco leaned forward as Osa rowed his boat around the low wharf that served the fishing village. Ahead of them stretched a broad length of beach on which a few boats had been careened for scraping and repairs. Lanterns glinted from the fishing boats as their owners prepared to sail. More people had gathered on the strand. Under a lantern dangling from a pole, a man sat cross-legged, testing the drum in his lap. A woman stood behind him, playing scales on a wooden flute.

"Your dad got *musicians?*" Pasco asked, goosebumps crawling over his back and arms. "For *me?*" He'll blame me when it doesn't work, Pasco thought, panicked. He'll say I promised I could dance a catch for him, and want me to pay these people!

"It's only my uncle and my cousin," Osa told him patiently. "Calm down. You jump worse than a landed cod."

Pasco made a face at his friend. The closer they got to the beach, the more he wished he'd said no when Osa first spoke of doing this.

You wanted to be paid for dancing, Pasco thought woefully, his breakfast a lead weight in his belly. Paid like a real dancer, like the ones who dance at festivals and for the duke, instead of just dancing at parties with your cousins and friends. And now it'll go bad, because you didn't have the backbone to refuse!

His mother had said it time after time, "You never think of consequences, Pasco. You just think about right now. One of these days the consequences will take you blind side in an alley, and you'll wonder how things got so bad." He pressed his face to his knees shivering.

Soon enough he felt the scrape of bottom under their keel. Strong hands grabbed the sides of the boat and dragged it up onto the beach.

"Come on, boy," a voice told him. Pasco looked up into the flinty eyes of Osa's grandmother. She wrapped a big-knuckled hand around his arm. "Take off your shoon. You got to learn this net-dance fast if you're to do it before we sail."

Men were working next to the flute player and drummer, laying something on the beach a corner at a time and securing it by staking it down. It was a real net, Pasco saw, one with bigger holes than most fishing nets. Hurriedly he stepped out of his shoes. Men and women left the boats to stand along the edges of the spread net, the lantern light rippling over their faces. They looked grim and forbidding, like statues of stern old gods.

"Two months 'thout enough fish to cover the deck," one of them muttered. "This better work."

Pasco's store of courage, never large, shrank even more as he looked at their faces. I'm dead, he thought weakly. I just ain't bothered to lay down yet.

"It's an easy step," Osa's grandmother told him. "Look at my feet, boy. I don't want to go repeating it. See, you dance each square of the net, like so." She was nimble in spite of her years, her feet tapping lightly on the sand to shape the four corners of a square. She did a light step over — "Next square, right in the middle," she explained to Pasco — her feet leaving a dent in the sand that would form its center. "Up one row of the net, down the next." Drummer and flute player were trying a lively tune that made Pasco think of leaping fish. Suddenly he was wide-awake. His feet were already tracing the sand pattern of steps without waiting for his head to decide to do it.

"Told you it was easy," the old woman said, watching his feet move. "You ready?"

He would have said he wasn't, not yet exactly, but the drummer and the flute player began that catchy tune in earnest, and his body wanted to dance. He stepped lightly into the first square on the net closest to him and marked the corners with his toes, his legs flicking across each other. It was a jig of sorts, and he always liked jigs. He locked his hands behind his back, keeping them firmly out of his way as the drum pounded and the flute trilled.

Square by square he called the fish, and he felt them answer, their tails flicking through the squares as his feet did. Oddly, his legs and feet were so warm they seemed almost fiery, though the warmth only came as high as his waist. It wasn't an uncomfortable warmth — if anything, it gave him strength.

When he finished, he did it by leaping from the last square and coming down, feet together, as light as any wisp of silk. The music stopped. He bowed to Osa's grand-mother, because it seemed like the right thing to do.

The sound of hands clapping made all of them, Pasco and the fisherfolk, turn. A party of riders had come onto the sand while Pasco was dancing.

Who was mad enough to be riding at this hour? Pasco wondered. He squinted at them, then gulped. His grace the duke of Emelan and the prettiest lady Pasco had ever seen were applauding him.

2

The lady dismounted from her horse and walked over. She was just an inch shorter than Pasco's own five feet five inches, but the way she held herself, back perfectly straight and head high, made her seem taller. She had a button of a nose, eyes of the brightest blue, and an open, friendly smile.

Blessed with four older sisters, Pasco took note of the lady's clothing. The girls would love to know she wore a pair of green breeches with legs so wide that, when she was afoot, she seemed to be wearing skirts. Over that she wore a long, sleeveless tunic in pale green cloth, fastened down the front with a row of tiny buttons shaped like suns. A full-sleeved blouse with green embroidery kept her arms from the cold. A sheer green silk veil was fixed somehow to light brown braids wound about the lady's head like a crown. She removed one of her tan riding gloves and offered him her bare hand.

Pasco took it and bowed, feeling a little dazed.

"You dance very well," she said with approval. "What is your name, please?"

Pasco could not reply. Osa's grandmother said respectfully, "He's Pasco Acalon, my lady. A friend of my grandson's." She dipped a quick curtsy and nudged Pasco with her elbow.

"Wha — ?" he asked, startled, and realized he still had the lady's hand in his. "I — I'm sorry. I didn't —" He dropped the small hand as if it had turned to fire.

"I thought I had seen nearly every kind of magic there is these last four years," the lady remarked in a friendly voice, "but never magic that was danced. Where did you learn it, Pasco?"

Now he gaped at her, flustered. "Magic? *Me,* do magic?" Magic was a thing of schools and books. No proper Acalon did magic. They were harriers. They had always been harriers, or the spouses of harriers, or the parents of harriers. "Oh, no — please, you're mistaken, my lady. I'm no mage."

She met his eyes squarely. "You just danced a magical working, Pasco Acalon. I am never mistaken about such things."

"Tell her," Pasco said pleadingly to Osa's grandmother. "You know I never had any sparkle of magic, not the tiniest."

"That he never did, my lady," admitted the old woman. "He and my grandson have been friends all their lives. There's nothing odd about Pasco. Just as ordinary as mud, 'less he starts showing more of a knack for harrier work."

"Not quite like mud, Gran," protested the boy Osa.

To Pasco's deep embarrassment, Osa told the lady — and by then, Duke Vedris, who had ridden over to listen — of the other times Pasco had danced for luck, and gotten what he'd danced for. Pasco stared at the sand, wishing he could just leap into one of the fishing boats now being launched.

When Osa finished, the duke leaned forward in the saddle. "Pasco Acalon — you are related to Macarin and Edoar Acalon?"

Pasco bowed to Duke Vedris. "My father and my grandfather, your grace."

"Then your mother was Zahra Qais before her marriage, and your maternal grandfather is Abbas Qais." The duke's quiet voice was soothing. With a smile he added, "Were all my servants as faithful and thorough as the Qaises and the Acalons of the Provost's Guard, I would be the most fortunate ruler on earth. My dear," he said to the young lady, "is it possible you are mistaken?"

"No, Uncle," the lady replied. She slid cool fingers under Pasco's chin and forced him to look up, to meet her eyes. "I didn't mean to startle you, but you do have power. If you didn't know it, then you need a teacher."

"My dear, before you began to rearrange his life, did you introduce yourself to this poor lad?" inquired the duke.

The lady stared up at him, startled, then started to grin. Quickly she bit on her lip until she was able to look at Pasco with a straight face. Her fingers never so much as twitched from their position under his chin. "I'm sorry. I'm used to everyone already knowing who I am. I'm Lady Sandrilene fa Toren, the duke's great-niece."

Pasco blinked at her for a moment, dazed. It was such a pretty name, as pretty as she was — then his mind began to work again. Sandrilene fa Toren. Any resident of Summersea over the last four years would know that name, and know it well. She was part of a quartet of young mages who had come to live in the temple city of Winding Circle, outside Summersea. First, they had managed to survive an earthquake while trapped underground. They had next destroyed a pirate fleet, then gone to the northern mountains to tame entire forests as they burned. They came back to the coast in time to help end the blue pox plague of 1036. Everyone told stories about them, including tales of the girl who wove bandages with the power to heal and veils that made the wearer as good as invisible. In a world in which mages were as common as architects or jewelers, Lady Sandrilene and her three friends were on their way to becoming great mages, the very best of their kind.

"Not meaning any disrespect, your ladyship," Pasco told her earnestly, "but maybe the magic's in the net. I'd've known if I was magic, 'deed I would." *My family would never let me hear the end of it*, he thought.

Her eyebrows, fine gold-brown crescents, rose. "You may not have," she replied firmly. "I didn't know until I was ten — just before I came here, in fact. My three friends didn't know until they came here, either, and Tris was inspected by a magic-finder. Some talents run very deep, Pasco Acalon. I think yours is one."

"Your grace!" A boy on a pony galloped onto the sand from the Harbor Road. He'd been riding hard: the pony was covered in sweat as they drew up next to Vedris's horse. The messenger wore the provost's colors. "They told me you rode this way," he gasped. "Captain Qais on dawn watch requests your grace's attendance at Rokat House, on Harbor Street."

Pasco frowned, thinking. This Qais would be his uncle Isman, who was not the man to send a boy out at full gallop without very good reason. Isman was so unflappable that if he were to see a tidal wave roaring down on him, he would blink and order his sergeants to find boats.

The duke and his great-niece traded looks. "And the nature of the emergency?" the duke asked coolly.

Perhaps Uncle Isman isn't the only one who'd take a

tidal wave in stride, thought Pasco, envious. That duke don't startle easy. Me, I'm like this messenger — too excitable.

"It's Jamar Rokat, the myrrh trader from Bihan, your grace," replied the messenger. "He's been murdered. It's a terrible sight, begging your grace's pardon."

Again the duke and his great-niece exchanged looks, the girl's startled, the duke's level. "Uncle," said Lady Sandrilene, reaching for the duke's reins.

He shook his head at her. "This is something that requires my attention, my dear. You have a problem of your own to solve just now."

She frowned up at him. "I suppose so, but —" She looked at Pasco, then back at her great-uncle.

The duke leaned down to cup her cheek in one hand and spoke too quietly for Pasco to hear. She replied, her voice just as soft; he spoke again. At last — very reluctantly, it seemed to Pasco — she nodded, and stood back. Immediately a man and a woman detached themselves from the squad of guards, moving their horses to stand by hers. They looked at Pasco, Osa, and Grandmother Netmender in a tough, memorizing way that Pasco knew very well. He'd seen it often enough on the faces of his own family: that habit of weighing people they'd met to decide who might be trouble, and who might not.

"Join me when you have concluded your business

here, Sandry," the duke told her. To the messenger he said, "Come along." He rode off, the boy and the squad of guards at his heels. A barrel-chested man who sported a sergeant's twin yellow arrowheads on his sleeve caught Sandry's eye and nodded to her before he followed the duke.

Pasco watched them go, thinking of what he'd overheard. Murder at Rokat House was a serious matter. He crossed his fingers and flicked them at the departing riders, sending luck for Uncle Isman in their wake. He would need all the luck he could get, particularly once Summersea's rich folk heard of the death of one of their own.

Sandry looked at Pasco thoughtfully as her uncle rode off. There were no two ways about it — something would have to be done with this boy. Untrained magic broke out in uncontrollable ways and could do considerable damage. She'd had that lesson drummed into her head over the past four years. From the glow of magic she'd seen as Pasco danced, his power wasn't such that it might flare up without warning, but that could change at any moment.

Sandry was no stranger to the ways of charming, clever boys. This one would bolt the moment he thought he could do so without offending a noble, and he wouldn't come back unless she did something to make him. Besides, she had the duke to think of. She did *not* want him putting his hard-won health in danger again, not on his first day outside Duke's Citadel.

"Murder at Rokat House," Pasco murmured. "That's got a jagged edge to it." How would Papa look into it? he wondered. Who might have done such a crime? There were all kinds of possibilities, as he knew from listening to the harriers in the family talk about their work. There were all sorts of angles to consider.

"How so?" asked Sandry. She needed to decide what she could do about the boy right at this moment and what she could put off to another, more convenient time.

"Only that Rokat House is the biggest importer of myrrh around the Pebbled Sea," Pasco explained, thinking aloud. Working it out as he'd been taught, he briefly forgot her nobility and her prettiness. "They're from Bihan, but they've houses in every big port. That's serious coin, and headaches for the harriers —"

"Harriers?" she interrupted. "What does that mean?"

"Provost's Guards are called harriers," he told her, still trying to remember his lessons on crime. "For the brown leather and the blue shirts they wear. Folk say it's a bit like some harrier hawks. And the watch-houses, in each district, they're called coops."

Sandry nodded, to show her understanding. This was an aspect of town life that she had never considered.

"Anyway, they got to get right to the case and catch

who done Jamar. Killed him, that is. The other Rokats here in Summersea'll be on his grace like pods on peas till the murderer's gathered up. Begging your ladyship's pardon." He yawned, and excused himself again. "Not that you need worry. Like as not, they'll have the killer in a cat's whisker."

Sandry looked at him, amused. "You sound very sure of that."

Pasco shrugged. "Mostways, a murderer's known to the one they killed — that's what my kinfolk say. Family, a friend. It's easy enough to track 'em down."

"So are you going to take up provost's work, too?" Sandry inquired.

The boy grimaced. "Both sides of my family are in it. It's not like I have a choice."

"If you were a mage, you'd have a choice," Sandry remarked slyly. If she could make learning magic attractive to him . . .

Pasco shook his head, his face set. "Lady, you don't know my family. The only kind of mage they'd want me to be is a harrier-mage, one that tracks blood back to the one that shed it. One that can lay a truth-spell on folk. I never heard of no harrier mages dancing what they do. I never heard of no dancing mages, either, not *ever*."

Sandry fidgeted. She had to catch up to her uncle. Before she could do that, she had to make this boy understand what had happened to him and his need for study. He didn't seem very convinced. If she could prove he was a mage, though, he would have to give in. "Make a bargain with me," she suggested.

"A bargain for what?" he asked warily.

"I'll meet you here, tonight, when the boats come in," she said. "If their catch is better than it's been in the last month or so, will you agree to talk some more about magic?"

He shook his head. "And I'm telling you, lady, you're plain mistook. I've got no magic."

Sandry frowned. "You say the word like it's a disease."

He bowed. "Beg pardon, lady. I meant no disrespect."

"Have we a bargain? We'll meet here tonight, and we'll see who has the right of it." If he'd had any training, he would have felt her magic hooking into his. With an invisible hand she teased out a strand of his power and pulled it to her, attaching it within herself. It was as fine as a single thread of silk, but with it in her grasp, she would always be able to find him. "Pasco, I want to catch up with my uncle," she said tartly. *Have we a bargain?*

He nodded reluctantly.

Sandry mounted her horse once again. Her guards drew up beside her, looking down at Pasco with level brown eyes. "Until the boats come home, Pasco Acalon," Sandry told him.

Again he bowed deeply to her.

Sandry nodded to her escorts, and turned her mare back toward the city. Once they reached the road, she set off at a smart trot, hoping to find the duke before he got too involved in this murder.

Pasco watched her ride off, shaking his head. He had little experience with nobles or mages, but he'd never heard of those people behaving as she did. Was she even as pretty as he'd thought, or was it just her bearing, and her dress, and those lovely blue eyes?

He oughtn't to meet her back here when the boats came in. Would a lady even know so commonplace a thing as the time a fishing fleet returned? If she didn't see him that afternoon, she would forget this idea of him and magery. Everyone knew the nobility was flighty, except for Duke Vedris.

Pasco looked around and found just Osa, napping beside his rowboat. Osa's father had gone off fishing without paying for the dance.

So I'll have to come anyway, to see if they still want to pay me, thought Pasco, wandering over to the sand where he'd danced. Dawn had come: in the sunlight he could see the patterns made by his feet and the rope net.

Pasco grinned. Suddenly the idea of an Acalon who danced magic was as funny as anything, a joke and a half.

"I have it," he told the air and a few seagulls that had

landed to pick for clams as the tide went out. "I'll be a dancing harrier, only 'stead of putting my hand on the lawbreakers, I'll — I'll dance 'em into my coop!"

"Are you done being foolish?" Osa demanded, getting to his feet. "I've chores to do yet today. And don't you have law and baton-fighting lessons?"

Pasco yelped, and ran to his friend. "No lessons till later," he told Osa, helping the other boy to push the boat into the water. "But I promised Mama I'd help sort one of the storerooms this morning!"

They jumped into the boat as it floated free. Each of them took an oar this time, and began to row.

When Harbor Street filled up with gawkers a block from the scene of the murder, Sandry's guards did not ask whether she wanted to push on or not. Like the other residents of Duke's Citadel, Kwaben and Oama had learned weeks ago what happened when Sandry wished to join her uncle and was kept from doing so. They urged their mounts ahead of hers and began to open a path with their booted feet and with their horses. People complained until they saw who barged through so rudely. Then they made room for the girl and her escort.

The four Provost's Guards at the door of Rokat House were less willing to help. Their leader, whose sleeve bore a corporal's single yellow arrowhead badge, was not impressed by Sandry's rank. "It's not a fit sight for a lady," he said, his face expressionless.

Oama dismounted so she could speak quietly to the man. "Corporal, think about this." She was a straightforward young woman with bronze skin, a long, straight nose, and sharp brown eyes, who wore her black hair rolled and pinned tightly at the back of her head. Her skills as a Duke's Guard and part of the elite Personal Guard were considerable: Sandry had watched her and her partner, Kwaben, at combat practice and had been impressed. "You don't want to vex her," Oama continued. *"Really."*

The corporal shook his head. "Captain Qais would boot me for it, and he'd be right."

Now Kwaben dismounted to support his partner. He was over six feet tall, black as sable, and honed like an axe. His shaved head, combined with sharp cheekbones, lean cheeks, and wide-set eyes, made him look as sleek and deadly as a panther. He was as dangerous as he appeared.

Sandry stayed on her mare. She would impress no one if she dismounted — the stubborn corporal was taller than she by a head. Instead she sorted through her magic until she found a particular cord. Shaped from her own power, it connected her to Duke Vedris.

"Uncle," she said clearly, feeling her voice roll down that magical tie, "I want to be let in, please."

Everyone stared at her, even Kwaben and Oama. Onlookers in the crowd drew the gods-circle on their chests. The Provost's Guards were made of sterner stuff. Their hands stayed by their weapons.

Overhead, on the next story of the building, glass

windows swung outward on hinges. The duke and a man with the same light brown skin, lean cheeks, and quirky eyebrows as Pasco leaned out.

"My dear, this is not the kind of thing a young girl should see," called Vedris. He could hear Sandry when she used the power she had bound to him, but without magic of his own he could not reply the same way.

Sandry looked up at him. He seemed tired, though she doubted anyone who did not know him well would guess that. He was also shaken, though that was something she felt rather than saw. "I'm no stranger to bad things, uncle. I really must insist."

Kwaben and Oama traded looks. They had heard her say that only once, on the day of the duke's heart attack, when his servants had tried to keep Sandry out of his room. After she had lost precious minutes in argument with them, she had finally insisted, in just that tone of voice. When they refused, every thread in the hall outside the duke's rooms — from tapestries, carpets, and even the servants' clothes — unraveled and came to life, cocooning them all. Sandry had gone to her uncle and had spent the rest of that day with the healers, keeping him alive with her magic until they could strengthen his heart. Kwaben and Oama had never forgotten it.

Now, leaning out of the second floor window, the duke grimaced. He knew that Sandry had seen things girls her age were supposed to be protected from: the bodies of hundreds, including her parents, rotting from plague; people dying in battle of human and magical causes; the survivors of fire, flood, and other disasters.

"Admit her," the duke said to his uniformed companion. The man began to argue as they closed the windows.

Sandry waited and tried not to drum her fingers on her saddle horn.

After a couple of minutes, the man who had tried to argue with the duke yanked open the door and spoke quietly to the guards. They looked at him, startled, then parted. The man, who wore a captain's pair of concentric yellow circles on his sleeve, waved Sandry in sharply.

She dismounted and passed her mare's reins to Kwaben. "Stay with the horses," she told her guards. "I think the rest of Uncle's escort are on that side street." They nodded.

The provost's captain stood aside as she walked into the building, then closed the door and lowered the thick oak bar that locked it. To her eyes door and bar gleamed with the pale traces of magic. So did the dimly lit hall that went to the rear of the building on this floor, and the narrow stair that reached the upper stories.

"Please reconsider, my lady," the man told her gruffly. "This is not an occasion for noble sightseers."

Sandry met his eyes. "You are Captain Qais?" she inquired.

He bowed stiffly.

"I will not reconsider," she said flatly. "My great-uncle has been ill. He tends to forget it, so I remember for him — and, it seems, for you. Where is he?"

"Upstairs, my lady."

Turning her back on him, Sandry climbed. The gleam of spell-signs lit her way; none of the stair lamps were burning. Since the captain didn't have her power to see magic, he missed the next step — they were uneven, to trick robbers into banging their toes just as he did. He cursed; when she looked back at him, he waved her on.

When she reached the top of the stairs, two hallways lay before her. One led to the rear of the building; the other cut across it. In the hall to her right, she saw only a flagstone floor, lamps in wall sconces, and closed doors. In the section to her left, the hall sported complexly patterned silk carpets — spelled, like everything else she had seen, with magic to protect and confuse anyone who was not allowed there. The lamps on this side were set in polished brass fixtures and circled with precious glass. Two mahogany benches were placed here. On them sat the three surly bodyguards who had attended Jamar Rokat earlier that morning, all in manacles. They looked confused, bewildered, and angry. Three Provost's Guards stood over them, baton weapons in hand.

"Why won't you believe us?" demanded the youngest of the three when he saw the captain. "We heard noth-

ing, nor saw it neither. He went in, the door was locked —
we never so much as heard a scream!"

"And the evidence shows you as liars," replied Captain
Qais. "You'll give up the facts when our truthsayers have
a go at you." To Sandry he said, "Why don't you wait for
his grace here?"

She walked ahead of him into the open room past the
captives. He mustn't know that she was nervous; she did
her best to hide it. She was no hardened — what had
Pasco called them — Harrier, that was it. She was not
one of those, but if her great-uncle was in this mess, that
was where she had to be as well.

Inside was a plain office belonging to Jamar Rokat's
secretary or assistant, it would seem. Sandry walked
through the open door at the back of the room into the
next office and halted. Her uncle sat on the window seat,
keeping out of the way of the Provost's Guards who were
going over the room inch by inch. They each wore the
silver braid trim on their sleeves that marked then as investigators, not street Guards.

There was blood everywhere. The hacked body of the
man who had greeted them so smoothly that morning
lay on the floor. His fine clothes were slashed and sodden
rags. His jewels lay in a bloody heap atop his desk, as if
whoever killed him had wanted to say they were too disgusting to steal. Worst of all, the man's head had been

placed in a sling made of his turban and hung from an overhead lamp.

A tiny woman in brown and blue stood by the dead man's feet, shaking her head. For all her small size, she had the lightly seamed face of someone in her fifties. "I can only guess they were waiting for him when he come in, cap'n, your grace," she said absentmindedly, staring at bloody slippers. "His guard spells never warned him."

"You can see from the furniture he never put up a fight," added another investigator as he went over a bookcase. "Even when his guards let them in. That don't make sense, 'less it was family done it."

"But the spells weren't released to let someone else in," Sandry blurted. Everyone looked at her. Sandry folded her hands. "Can any of you see or feel magic?" They all shook their heads. "Most spells like this, if you can see them, they turn colors, depending on whether someone broke through, or tried to erase them, or just released their effects for a while. Using a password just releases — it halts the protections, it doesn't end the spell. And *this*" — she waved a hand to take in the spells all around them — "it hasn't been touched. I can tell that just by looking at it. Even though Rokat wasn't a mage, he'll have owned a key to these spells. He would have been able to look at that and know their status. The keys are usually made like jewelry —"

"Here." A sergeant whose almond-shaped eyes and gold skin showed his ancestors were from the Far East went to the desk. He used a wooden rod drawn from a quiverlike container hung on his belt to separate a piece of jewelry from the sticky heap of gems and precious metal. It was a long oval pendant on a chain. "Don't touch it, my lady," he cautioned. "Not till our mages have a go at it. We knew he had spells on the place, of course, though we can't see them. His kind always does."

She nodded and leaned closer. The pendant was inlaid with a number of minute squares, each made of black, pale, or fire opal. A thin slice of clear crystal was laid over them. A hair-fine thread of magic stretched away from each square. "He would have paid a fortune for this," Sandry murmured. "Yes, it's his key. Each square must be tied to a different set of spells, so he'd know exactly *where* somebody tried to break in. But *look* at it." She glanced at the Guards and their captain, all of whom stared at her without understanding. There was a tiny, ironic smile on the duke's lips. He gave her a slight nod. "Like I said, the spells were never touched. This whole pendant is dark," Sandry told them. "Nothing's glowing, and it's made to be read by someone with no magic whatever. *No one* broke through these spells."

"The killers' spells were better, that's all," said Captain Qais bluntly. "Someone always has better magic. Or the guards, or one of the family, must have given the right passwords to whoever they let in."

"But we had no trouble comin' in *without* passwords," the tiny woman pointed out.

"You had no trouble because Jamar Rokat is dead," Sandry replied. "The main power of the spells would be keyed to him."

The duke rubbed his chin. "Surely after he went to the expense to have these spells laid on, he'd only give passwords to a few. He was a careful man with many enemies. He'd keep the password to this room for his own use."

"Coulda come in over the roof," said the bald, chunky man who was the third investigator.

"He'd've spelled the roof, too," the sergeant told them tersely. "*He* never left no loopholes, not him."

Sandry looked at the ceiling, though she was really inspecting the magical fabric above it. There were storerooms on the floors upstairs, all with their own protections. The roof was a solid mass of untouched magic. She shook her head. "You're right. The roof is absolutely covered with spells, and none show signs of tampering."

Captain Qais crossed his arms. "Begging your pardon, your ladyship, but you are versed in weaving and needlework. We have mages who know just this kind of thing, magic used by criminals and magic used to keep criminals out. They will be able to explain. And I still think those guards will talk plenty once they're sweated."

Sandry stared at the man, honestly shocked. What did he think magic was, if not a kind of thread? He spoke as though she'd spent the last four years minding a spinning wheel or a tapestry frame, not cudgeling her brain with lessons in arts, sciences, and the theories of how and why mages could get magic to work.

"Captain," the duke said coolly, "if your mages are coming, we must not remain underfoot." He got up. "You will keep me apprised of all developments?"

The captain was studying Jamar's head. He glanced at the duke, startled at the interruption, and hurriedly bowed. "Of course, your grace."

Sandry hesitated. She would like to see Provost's Mages — whom Pasco had called "harrier-mages." They would be academic mages, taught at places like the university in Lightsbridge, their ways different from those of craft-mages like Sandry and her friends. While she had been taught academic methods and had learned about different specialties in academic magic, she had never seen a Provost's Mage at work.

The duke offered Sandry his arm. She had a choice, she realized — she could stay, or she could get her uncle back to Duke's Citadel. Her uncle came first, so she took the offered arm. Perhaps she could get him to introduce her to some Provost's Mages before she went home to Winding Circle.

Sandry and the duke made their way out of the building in silence. Two of the guards stationed before the door escorted them to their horses and their own soldiers. Sandry kept a wary eye on the press of human beings that folded away from them, but there were no weapons in the fingers that brushed the duke's tunic or arm and there was only respect in the whispers of "Gods bless your grace."

Their approach was so quiet that they surprised one of the Duke's Guard telling some Provost's Guards, "— took an *hour* to cut them out of her cocoons. They growed into the very walls and floor —"

Someone cleared her throat and the guards snapped to attention. Their mounts were brought forward as the Provost's Guards melted back through the side door to Rokat House.

"Some got nothing better to do than gossip," Kwaben said to no one in particular.

Sandry peered at her uncle and saw the corner of his mouth quiver with amusement. She almost smiled herself. Perhaps it was bad of me, she thought as she mounted her horse. Still, at least I taught them who they're dealing with. No one will keep me away from Uncle again.

Once in the saddle, there was a delay while the duke

spoke to their guard sergeant. The knowledge of what she'd seen in that building hit Sandry without warning. The copper stink of blood returned to her nose; the sight of a man she'd met with his head cut off lingered in her mind's eye. She gripped her saddle horn with hands that trembled. For once in her life she wished passionately that she carried smelling salts, or even a scented ball as some nobles did, to clear her nose and chase off the shudders.

A brown hand wrapped around an open water bottle entered her vision. Oama had brought her mount up close to Sandry's. "It's all right," she told the girl quietly. "It's just water with a bit of lemon for cleaning out the mouth."

Sandry drank and returned the bottle with a shaky smile.

"Was it bad?" Oama asked softly.

Sandry nodded.

"We reap what we sow," murmured the duke. He had finished his conversation with the sergeant. "It sounds cold," he told Oama and Sandry, "but Jamar Rokat sent enough people into the next world before their rightful time that he must have known someone might grant him the same." The duke patted Sandry's arm. "Ready to go?"

She nodded.

*   *   *

The moment they clattered into the inner courtyard of Duke's Citadel, the seneschal, Baron Erdogun fer Baigh, walked briskly out of the duke's residence and down the steps. He was a whippet-lean man with light brown skin and brown eyes set under a cliff of forehead. Above that he was as bald as an egg; what little black hair remained on the sides of his head was cropped painfully short. He was fussy, precise, and arrogant, but he was devoted to Vedris, which countered his flaws as far as Sandry was concerned.

"Your grace, I had begun to worry if some accident had befallen you," he said, bowing. He hovered as Vedris dismounted, but like Sandry, he had learned not to help.

"We would have sent word of an accident, Erdo," replied the duke. "There was a problem, of course. Jamar Rokat was murdered this morning."

"Good riddance to bad rubbish," the baron said crisply. He fell in half a step behind the duke as Vedris began to climb the residence steps.

"I need to return to the fishing village this afternoon," Sandry told Oama and Kwaben. "Meet me here at three?"

They bowed to her from the saddle and took the reins of her mare. Sandry ran to catch up with the duke and Baron Erdogun. The baron was saying, "— and your plans for the remainder of the morning?"

The duke sighed. "I believe I will lie down until lunch."

Two weeks before, when he was allowed to leave his quarters and go downstairs, they had set up a couch for him in one of the parlors opening into the entrance hall. It said a good deal for how tired he was that he simply walked into the ground floor parlor and shut the door.

Erdogun turned on Sandry, his hands on his hips. "He just happened to stop by a murder?" he asked tartly.

"There was nothing I could do about that," Sandry informed him. "You know how he is."

Erdogun sighed and rubbed his bald crown. "The mail's arrived," he said. It wasn't his nature to apologize for being sharp, as Sandry had already found. "I honestly don't know what to tell Lord Frantsen anymore."

Sandry didn't like the duke's ambitious oldest son. They had met in the past, and since the duke's heart attack the tone of Frantsen's letters had grown arrogant — as if he had already inherited. "Tell him and that grasping wife of his that Uncle cut them from his will."

The parlor door opened. "Don't think it hasn't crossed my mind," the duke said quietly. The door closed again.

"Wonderful," Erdogun muttered and stalked down the hall to the large workroom from which he oversaw affairs at Duke's Citadel.

Sandry followed him wearily. She missed her old life, before she had found herself watching the health of a man who didn't want to be fussed over and dealing with a hundred retainers, each more prickly than the last.

She thought dreamily of Discipline cottage at Winding Circle. By this time her teacher Lark would be at her loom, at work on her newest creation. She even envied Pasco: by now he must be sauntering through the marketplace with his friends, without a care in the world.

"Pasco!" The padded end of a baton thumped the side of his head firmly enough to make him stagger. "Scorch it all, boy, pay attention! Knowing the baton might save your silly skull in a dark alley one day!" Exasperated with her youngest child, Zahra Acalon pushed a lock of dark, wavy hair out of her face. She was a tall woman in her late thirties, handsome rather than pretty, with strong black brows, dark eyes, and a wide, decided mouth. Sweat glued her cotton shirt to her back. Impatiently she twitched the cloth away from her chest, flapping it slightly to cool her skin. "If I've told you once, I've told you a hundred times —"

"Daydreams will be my death," he said along with her. "Sorry, Mama."

"Pasco got thu-umped, Pasco got thu-umped," sang his cousin Rehana wickedly. Five of the residents of House Acalon who were Pasco's age or a little older had gathered in the courtyard. There his mother Zahra taught them the Provost's Guards' traditional weapons — staff, baton, weighted chain — and hand-to-hand combat.

"I'll thump *you*, Reha," Pasco muttered out of the side of his mouth.

A baton tapped him under the chin. "Learn to keep from being thumped yourself, before you deal out knocks of your own," his mother advised. "And the rest of you, you aren't doing so well that you can torment him."

Fast as a snake, she whirled and swung overhand at Reha. The girl blocked her strike with her baton, almost as quick as Zahra herself. With her attention on that descending baton, Reha did not see Zahra reach out with a booted leg and hook the girl's feet from under her. Down Reha went, still remembering to keep her own baton between her and any attack from overhead.

"Well enough," Zahra said with approval. "But look at the weapon just long enough to tell its direction. Your main attention should have been on my chest. My body's movement there would have warned you of my kick."

"Fat chance," muttered Reha.

Zahra grinned evilly at her. "Perhaps not." She swept their small group with her eyes. "The point of all this is to make sure you come home from your watch alive. To do that you have to *pay attention*. Live the moment you're in. Stay open to all the things around you, be they smell, sound, or sight —"

Her baton flashed up and to the side. This time Pasco was ready — he'd seen the muscles in Zahra's legs, outlined by her breeches, shift. He blocked her with his baton and grabbed her wrist with his free hand. Twisting it, he dragged her down and across his body. Once she was facedown on the ground, he shoved the arm he had captured up behind her back. Half-kneeling, he pressed one knee into his mother's spine.

"I could've fought the takedown, boy," she said, her voice muffled by the bricks of the courtyard.

Pasco released her. "I know, Mama." When she struggled to rise, he offered her a hand. She took it and in a heartbeat he went flying.

Tucking himself into a ball, he unfolded and struck feet first, skidding to a halt before he smacked into the columned gallery that ran around the edge of the courtyard. Rising on tiptoe, he gave her his fool's bow, the one that was much too deep. Straightening, he rose to the very top of his toes, stumbled forward as if he were out of control, then flipped in the air and came back to his feet, arms spread.

Zahra glared at him. "Was that meant to charm your way out of a drubbing?" she wanted to know.

Pasco bowed his head. "I live to be drubbed," he said meekly.

She could only be cross with him for so long. "Get your baton. All of you, line up. We'll do the patterned strike-and-block combinations until time for midday."

Pasco shook his black hair out of his eyes and took the baton Reha held out to him. "Say, Mama, did you ever hear of magic dancing? Well, mages that dance, and the dancing is a spell."

"Ridiculous," Zahra said flatly. "Take your place in line, *now*."

Pasco did as ordered. As his mother called off the movements of the combinations, he concentrated on that, at least until the midday bell rang.

As the young people washed up before eating, Pasco's cousin Haidaycie elbowed him. "When are you going to grow up?" she demanded. "Dancing *magic*, Pasco, of all things! What's next? Dancing a fortune into our pockets?"

"Come on, Haiday. He'll say anything to get the family to let him play tippy-feet with half-naked dancing girls," jeered one of his older male cousins, Vani. "It beats *working* for his supper."

"The sooner you face facts, the happier you'll be," Reha informed Pasco with all the wisdom of her sixteen years. "You're an Acalon and a Qais. Harrying is your life."

"There's plenty of Acalons and Qaises who aren't harriers!" argued Pasco.

They all looked at him as if to say, *Don't waste our time.*

"If you ever want a say in the family, you'll go for harrier," Haiday informed him as she dried her hands.

"She's right," said Reha. "Besides, you're Macarin's

and Zahra's only son. You *have* to harry." She followed Haiday inside.

"Tippy-feet," jeered Vani. He flicked his drying-cloth at Pasco hard, lashing the younger boy's cheek.

Pasco yelped. Holding the weal left by the cloth, he glared at Vani as the older boy ambled into the house. Someday, Pasco told himself, he would make Vani pay for all his towel-flicking.

The duke emerged from his parlor, looking better, and joined Sandry and Baron Erdogun for lunch. After that, they all applied themselves to the affairs of Duke's Citadel and the realm. In the weeks after the duke's heart attack, when he had rested all afternoon, Erdogun and Sandry fell into the habit of meeting in a nearby study to deal with the work that built up. In the quiet afternoon hours, Sandry took the household accounts over from Erdogun, with his blessing. It gave her something useful to do and gave him less work.

Once the duke grew well enough for Healer Comfrey to agree that a little business would not tax him, he joined Sandry and Erdogun for an hour, then two, then three. When it was judged that he was strong enough to leave the second floor and go downstairs, they set up a workroom there. The baron labored over heaps of documents while the duke read reports and Sandry attended to the running of a large castle. Often the duke and Erdogun discussed matters involving Emelan and met with various officials. Many times they asked Sandry's opinion. They explained it as wanting the views of a mage or another noble, but Sandry wondered if the duke wanted to see how her mind worked. She couldn't imagine why he might want her ideas on the proper scale of punishments for theft, but she respected as well as loved him and answered him as seriously as she could.

The afternoon that followed Jamar Rokat's murder sped by. All too soon it was time for Sandry to meet Pasco at the fishing village. Oama and Kwaben awaited her with her mare, Russet, when she emerged from the residence. Riding through the city in mid-afternoon was a slower matter than at dawn. There were horses and wagons to be got around, stray animals, and all kinds of people. The talk on every corner seemed to be about the merchant's very messy death.

She had meant to be early for the fishers' return, but to her surprise most of the boats were home and in the process of unloading their contents. Each crew had brought in as much fish as their boats might carry. The entire village had turned out to help load baskets of fish into carts that would take them to the city for sale.

Pasco Acalon stood on the beach, his jaw hanging open.

Sandry drew rein beside him. "Now do you believe you have magic?" she asked.

He started with surprise — he had not heard her ride up — and bowed hastily. "Lady, my mother has never heard of dancing mages. She was once a captain of the Provost's Guard. If she never heard of a thing, then how can it exist? This, this was just luck, pure and simple. It had to turn sometime. Whatever drove the fish off —"

A burly man in fisherman's clothes strode toward them, a grin on his dark face. He grabbed Pasco's hands and folded them around a leather pouch. "Well, lad, you did the trick." He looked at the boats, shaking his head. "This day's work puts food on our plates through Death's Night, once it's smoked. And Gran says the charm holds till the next full moon — enough to make up what we've lost this year." He thumped Pasco on the shoulder, bowed quickly to Sandry, then strode back toward the workers.

The boy poured the contents of the bag into his palm and gasped. "Five silver crescents!" he cried. "Master Netmender, you said only one crescent!"

"It's bad luck to underpay a mage," the fisherman called back over his shoulder. "Just don't get greedy next year! Hi, Osa, be careful with that basket!"

"Mage?" whispered Pasco. "Next *year?*"

"Well?" Sandry asked the boy, nudging him with a

booted foot as he continued to stare at the boats. "I know magic when I see it. So do these people. You need proper training, before your power starts breaking out in ways you don't want it to. And it will. Power's funny that way."

"Power or none, it don't matter, lady," Pasco said gloomily. "You don't know my family, begging your pardon. If I was a harrier-mage, that would please them no end — but even if there *is* such a thing as dancing magic, it's still *dancing*, get it? The moon'll drop plumb out of the sky afore my family lets me dance for my supper."

"Explain it to them," Sandry told him firmly, trying to keep her growing impatience hidden. She supposed he'd been through a lot today, but surely he could see what was right under his nose. He acted as if he were to ignore his power long enough, it would go away. "Surely they must have noticed something odd about you by now."

"Other than me not having the sense of a butterfly?" Pasco inquired, meeting her eyes. The curl of his mouth was bitter. "They've noticed *that*, right enough. But no one's said anything to me of magic. I never saw pictures in the fire or made things dance in the air when I was a babe, like all the mages do —"

"I didn't," Sandry told him flatly. "Any more than my friends did." Pasco winced and she sighed. Where had people gotten this silly notion that Briar, Daja, and Tris were to be feared? "Not all magic shows itself like that," she went on.

He looked from her to the boats, black eyes wide with panic, then shook his head and clapped his hands to his ears. Still covering them, he bowed and walked away, toward Summersea's east gate.

"Shall I fetch him back, my lady?" asked Oama. "Knock sense into that head?"

"No, please don't," Sandry replied. "He's frightened, that's all. Besides, I'll be able to find him when I need to." Thinking it over, she knew she was in over her head. She hadn't the first notion of what to do next, but she knew who would.

"I have to go to Winding Circle," she told her guards.

Once inside the curtain wall that sheltered the temple city of Winding Circle, Sandry told Oama and Kwaben to ride to the east gate stables, where they and their mounts would be made comfortable until Sandry was ready to go home. They insisted on remaining with her until she had dismounted in front of the small cottage that lay behind the Earth temple. Only then did they take her mare's reins and leave.

The cottage known as Discipline was set back from the temple's spiral road and framed in gardens. For a moment Sandry remained outside the gate, looking around her. She had left in a hurry, hoping to be back in a day or two. Now she felt like a stranger. She had not helped to whitewash the cottage, weatherproofing it against the winter storms. She had not helped to put a fresh layer of thatch on the roof, or to bring in the last fruits and vegetables. The shutters on her room and the rooms of her three friends were tightly shut, as they had almost never been when the four were there.

Lark must be so lonely with no one at home, Sandry thought sadly. That spring Tris, Briar, and Daja had left Winding Circle with their teachers, who had decided they needed to see more of the world and of the magics used outside the temple city. Sandry and Lark had rattled about the empty cottage all summer, until word had come of the duke's heart attack. It had been just like Lark to urge Sandry to go and stay with her great-uncle for as long as was necessary.

Sandry shook her head. She had seen Lark since the duke's illness, but always at the citadel. This was her first trip home, and she felt as if she'd lost something. She missed open shutters, the sight of Briar's miniature pine in his window, the lamps burning in the workshops built onto the sides of the cottage. Something else was missing, too.

Opening the gate, she realized what it was. Once any visitor would be hailed by canine shrieks and then bowled over, if they were not careful, by the wolfhound-sized dog who lived here — Little Bear was enthusiastic in his greetings. He belonged to all four of the young people. That spring, when Tris's teacher Niko wanted to take her south, Tris had been so heartbroken at leaving that they had talked her into taking the dog. The three of them would be south of the Pebbled Sea by now, and were not due to return until next summer.

The front door was closed against the night's growing chill. Sandry, feeling unsure, knocked.

She heard footsteps, then the door opened. The woman who stood there was four inches taller than Sandry, with bronze-colored skin and wide brown eyes set over sharp cheekbones. Lark was dressed in a long habit of the dark green shade worn by those who dedicated themselves to the gods of the earth. She smiled warmly and hugged Sandry. "What a wonderful surprise!" she exclaimed. "I wasn't expecting to see you till next week! How is his grace? Come in, and we'll have tea."

Sandry hugged Lark fiercely, then walked into her home.

Once she had brewed some tea, Lark made Sandry relax and eat. As she did, Sandry asked after the other residents of Winding Circle. "I have to stay with Uncle a while more," she said, though Lark hadn't asked when she would be coming home. "Till I'm *sure* he'll be all right. He was so tired this morning, and he doesn't know how to be careful."

Lark smiled at her. "It's comforting to know you're with him," she said, offering Sandry an apple. "He really does listen to you — he has ever since we took that

55

trip north with him, the year when you first came to us. He told us then he thought you had a head on your shoulders. And everyone knows he works much too hard."

Looking at her made Sandry feel as if she'd been walking through a gale and had stepped through a door into a warm house. "I miss you so much," she said. "I wish you were there with me."

Lark shook her head. "I have so much to do here. Besides, Duke's Citadel is too big and drafty for an ex-tumbler turned stitch witch," she teased. "And Dedicate Vetiver says one of the novices who came this summer shows some odd flashes that could be magic. I don't think Daja will mind if this boy turns out to need her old room. Vetiver says he's terribly shy and can hardly speak, even to other novices."

Sandry nodded. Just-discovered mages who had trouble fitting in at Winding Circle were often turned over to Lark and Rosethorn. The two women had taught a number of mages over the years, though none so unusual as Sandry, Briar, Daja, and Tris. "Can you manage without Rosethorn here?" asked Sandry.

Lark chuckled. "It might even be easier, at least for the first few months. Never tell Rosie I said that."

Sandry grinned. Dedicate Rosethorn was a terror.

The Hub clock chimed the hour. It was getting late,

and there was the ride back to Duke's Citadel to be thought of. "Lark, this boy I found . . ." She told her teacher about Pasco. "His magic's as plain as the nose on my face," she said when she had finished. "I'm just not sure of what to do. Should I leave him to his own devices? We were always told that if a mage doesn't get proper training, sooner or later his magic starts to run wild, like Tris's used to." Her friend Tris had left a wake of frightened people and ruined property before she had come to Discipline.

Lark sat back in her chair, brows knit in thought. "A dance-mage," she murmured. "How very odd."

"I figured you'd know if there were any," Sandry pointed out. "All the places you've been."

Lark rubbed her temples. "I've seen a few, but it was far and away. The shamans of the Qidao people dance their magic. So do the shamans of Ugurulz — it's between the Sea of Grass and Yanjing, in the north."

"He won't go all that way to learn from a shaman if he doesn't even want his magic here," Sandry remarked. "What about those Qidao people?"

"More thousands of miles," Lark replied. "They're in southern Yanjing. Even if he wanted to journey so far, we couldn't allow it. First he must learn basic control over his power. There's no telling what kind of mischief he could set in motion with a step here, and a step there."

"I don't think he's strong enough to do serious damage," Sandry told her.

"It doesn't matter if he is or he isn't," Lark said. "Dances are patterns. You know what patterns can do."

"Placing magic in a pattern makes the magic stronger," Sandry replied; it was a lesson she knew as well as her own name. She smiled. "That's why you and I have to be careful when we weave. So you're saying that Pasco can extend his power through dance patterns."

"Easily." Lark toyed with her teacup. "And the stronger the pattern, the more things can go wrong. What if this Pasco had not followed the net so faithfully? A wrong step that broke the net magic might have driven all the fish from the sea for miles. What if he'd thought of pretty girls as he danced? He could have called all the girls of Summersea to him, whether they wished to be called or not. You're absolutely right. Pasco must be taught."

"So I'll bring him to the school here." Sandry felt better immediately: a decision had been reached.

Lark shook her head. "It's not that simple. Temple and university mages follow laws and guidelines, some of which you know. On the subject of new mages, the law is set. If no teacher with the same power is available, the discovering mage has to teach the newcomer the basics."

Sandry laughed. "But the discovering mage is *me*."

Lark nodded gravely.

"I'm just a kid myself," Sandry pointed out, using street slang for child. "I can't teach him. I have to keep an eye on Uncle."

"You can and you must teach," said Lark firmly. "The Winding Circle Initiate Council or the mage council at the university in Lightsbridge enact penalties on a mage who shirks her responsibility."

Sandry sat bolt upright in her chair. "And if I do not recognize their authority?" she demanded, offended by the idea that these strangers might try to control her life.

Lark laid a hand over hers. "If you did not follow the rules, then as a great mage of the Winding Circle Initiate Council it would be my task to teach you your duty."

Sandry blinked at her. She knew that Lark — and Rosethorn, when she was home — often attended what they always referred to as "council meetings." She had always assumed they were meetings of the Dedicate Council that governed the temple city, not a council of temple mages.

"Mages without law are dangerous," Lark said. "What if there were no duke to rule in Emelan? If he just vanished, with no heir appointed?"

"Someone else would take his position," replied Sandry hesitantly. It hurt her heart to think of it.

"After bloodshed," Lark pointed out. "After civil war. Mage councils ensure that our people have someone to answer to, as Emelan answers to his grace. Other parts of the world have their own ways to hinder rogue mages."

"I don't know *how* to teach," complained Sandry.

"It hasn't been that long since you learned the basics," Lark said firmly. "Start with those. Go through your uncle's library. Talk to merchants and nobles — see if any of them have ever heard of dance-mages. And he'll need a dance teacher. If he's from a lower-class family, he'll know jigs, country dances, and wedding dances, but little else. Learning new dances will help to keep him out of mischief, and create a direction for his power." Bending down, she picked her workbasket up from the floor. It was filled with clothes — she dumped them on the table. "If you'll take the stitching out, I'll cut these into patches for a quilt," she told Sandry. "One of the East District families wants the father to have a quilt made of their old things when he takes ship in the spring."

"That's sweet," remarked Sandry, pulling a tattered shirt toward her. Turning it inside out, she laid her fingers along one of the seams and called to the thread that held it closed. The thread began to wriggle free, twining around her index finger like a vine. Watching it slither out of the cloth, Sandry remembered the most vexatious part of her conversations with Pasco.

"He seems to think his family won't let him learn magic," she pointed out to Lark, drawing out the threads that tacked the cuffs to the shirt. "He says it would be different if he had a talent for provost's magic, but his family won't hear of dancing magic — as if it's a toy that Pasco might pick up. I don't understand it."

"You see this in a lot of guild families and in the noble houses," Lark replied, cutting a worn skirt into squares. "And from what I heard of the Acalons when I lived in the Mire, they've served the provost for generations. They're practical people. Still, they aren't fools. Once they realize Pasco is a genuine mage, they'll know he must be taught." She put her scissors down and gazed at Sandry. "Of course, they may take it better if they hear it from you."

The girl sighed. The last thread came out of the collar, leaving the shirt in pieces on the table before her. She stacked them up and put them aside, drawing a pair of breeches out of the pile. "I really think he should be the one to tell them. He might as well get in the habit of owning up to his magic, after all." Once she had turned the breeches inside out, she saw these were better made than the shirt, with the ends of the thread all hidden inside the hems. She glared at the cloth. All the sewing-threads jumped out of the material in a hundred pieces, flying across the room.

Lark hid a smile behind her hand and remarked quietly, "That seems like a dreadful waste of thread."

Sandry nodded wryly, and lifted her hands. It took several calls to get the scattered pieces to return. Once she had them, she scooped them into a mound on the table. She petted them gently for a moment until they ceased to tremble. When the bits of thread were calm, she sent her power cautiously through each fiber. As the mound wriggled and shifted, she confessed, "I don't know how I'm going to get him to *like* the idea of magic."

"Of course you do," Lark said, picking up a square of cloth in one hand and her scissors in the other. "It sounds like your Pasco is dying to dance. Lure him in by telling him he gets to learn new dances to use with his power. Of course, he'll have to practice a great deal — but I'll wager he wants to practice dancing. You just need to weave the two lessons into one, and I know you can do that."

Sandry looked up at her teacher and grinned. She had a feeling Lark was exactly right. "Are you *sure* someone else can't teach him?" she asked, though she was fairly certain of the answer.

Lark grinned back at her. "It seems to me that teaching will be a very good discipline for you, too," she replied, mock-serious. "Mila knows it was good for me."

"Was it hard, teaching magic?" Sandry wanted to know.

Lark nodded. "But I was older than you, and much

more set in my ways," she pointed out. "And I was so new to my own magic, coming to it late as I did, that I was convinced I was leaving out something important. I'll tell you what Vetiver told me: don't forget that Winding Circle is nearby. If you get stuck, ask questions." She gathered up her scraps and put them aside. "Personally," she added, "I think Pasco is very lucky to have you for a teacher. I think you're going to be very good at it."

"I only hope I'm as good as you one day," Sandry remarked softly. "You were so patient with me."

Lark shook her head. "You give me too much credit. It was very easy to be patient with you, and an absolute joy to teach you."

Sandry looked down, blushing with pleasure. Hearing that from Lark meant a great deal to her. Lark was pleasant, but she also didn't believe in compliments unless they were earned.

When Sandry checked the heap of thread-bits, she saw they had woven themselves into one strand. Now they arranged themselves in a polite coil, as if they wanted to show Sandry they could behave. "Thank you," she told them. "You did that very nicely, and I'm sorry I frightened you before."

She didn't notice Lark's smile. She was thinking, Thread minds me — why can't Pasco? That wasn't entirely fair, and she knew it. This thread came from sheep, who were docile enough if you kept after them. Silk thread would have been harder to control, since the caterpillars that spun silk worked only for themselves.

Remembering her friend Briar at Pasco's age, Sandry wondered if he'd been as deliberately ignorant as Pasco was this afternoon. Briar hadn't been. He could be infuriating, and difficult, and independent, but he was also a realist. He would never argue when someone had pointed out something obvious, like his magic. That made her wonder, was it Briar who'd been unusual for his age, or the boy she had met today?

"Pasco seems so *young*," she complained. "But that's impossible. He's two years older than any of us were at the start of our studies."

"But by then you in particular were no longer young," Lark told her quietly.

Sandry looked down. She knew what Lark meant. Two weeks locked in a cellar in a country gone mad, with her parents and nursemaid dead and no hope of Sandry's ever being found, had worked a change on her ten-year-old self. The weeks she had spent afterward, staring at a ceiling and not wanting to leave her bed, had done still more to age her past her years.

"Give me a day or two," Lark suggested. "I'll ask some of the dancers I know to recommend a teacher — someone who won't be unnerved if Pasco's control over his power slips." Lark still kept the performer friends she'd made in her youth, before she took her vows. "In the meantime, begin his lessons in meditation as soon as possible. And be prepared to talk to his parents."

Sandry nodded gloomily. She didn't feel at all confident about teaching.

Lark came over and gave her a hug. "The wheel turns," she told Sandry. "The student becomes the teacher. And you'll do me credit — just you wait and see."

Sandry chuckled and returned the hug. "If I can do half as well as you, I'll count myself lucky."

5

Once baton practice started, it was a good idea to think about only baton practice, not about full nets or Lady Sandrilene. Pasco's mother Zahra was feeling brisk: she made them all step lively that morning. The cousins' feet slapped the courtyard tiles as if they were step dancers all doing the same measures.

When a maid told Zahra someone had come to see her, Zahra ordered them to pair up and practice the latest drill. The moment she was gone, Pasco and a couple of the others sat down to rest.

A baton thumped Pasco's crown. "You heard your mama, tippy-feet," his cousin Vani said, jeering. "Come prance around with me a bit."

Pasco replied with a rude suggestion.

Vani growled, and rapped Pasco's head again. Pasco saw stars.

"Stop it, Vani," Reha protested. "You'd be cleaning chamberpots for weeks if Aunt Zahra saw that."

"She won't catch me, though, and you won't tell if you're wise." Glaring at Pasco, Vani added, "Guess who got stuck hauling wood this morning while somebody took his sweet time coming back from market? Wha'd you do, Pasco? Stop and goggle at them Capchen dancers practicing in the yard at Wainwright's inn?" Vani banged Pasco's knees, then his shins, with his baton.

Pasco surged to his feet and lunged at Vani, baton out. His cousin backed away, swung his weapon and knocked Pasco's from his grip. He surveyed Pasco with narrowed eyes. "I got to teach you not to stick me with all the hot sweaty work."

Pasco trembled. Vani was going to hurt him again. Even if one of the girls fetched help, sooner or later Vani would get his revenge. For some reason Pasco brought out the worst of Vani's mean streak. Now he shrank back, raising his hands to guard his face as his bigger cousin drew close.

A bit of flute music threaded through his mind. The Capchens had danced to it. . . .

Humming the tune, Pasco took three quick steps to the right, his arms in the air, palm-to-palm overhead.

Vani halted and rolled his eyes. "*Now* what?" he demanded.

Pasco took another three quick steps to the left. He lowered his arms halfway, holding them like wings out from his sides. He arched his chest, head high. Long step next, then *leap* at Vani, one leg bent, the other trailing straight behind him.

Vani, Haiday, and the youth behind them flew up and back as if thrown. Pasco landed on the ground and waited for them to do the same.

They didn't. All three stayed in the air, four feet above the tiles. They hung, and they hung, and they hung.

"Pasco, what did you do?" breathed Reha, who was earthbound. "That *was* you, wasn't it?"

"No," he said quickly.

The three hanging Acalons flailed without shifting their bodies an inch. "Let me down!" yelled Vani. "Right now, you puling, puking little rat turd!"

Pasco licked his lips. Time. He needed time to think. "Promise you won't beat me up," he retorted, his voice squeaking.

"I'll mince you is what I'll do! Get me down!"

Reha left the courtyard and returned with a tall stool. She thrust it under Haiday, as if she just needed a step down. Haiday struggled, but the air held her fast. Reha tried the stool on the other two, without result.

Vani kicked it over when she put it under him. "Pasco, get me down or you're hog food!"

"Promise," whispered Pasco, mind racing like a panicked mouse. All he could think was that Vani would need to hurry to beat Mama to killing him.

A sharp voice demanded, "What is going on out here? You children know very well Great-grandmother rests at this hour!" Gran'ther Edoar walked out of his quarter of the house, as cross as a bear. Leaning on his walking stick, the tall old man went up to the three hanging Acalons and tugged Haiday's leg. She remained in the air.

Pasco fell to his knees with a whimper.

Gran'ther walked around the three, looking them over, pulling first an arm, then a leg. Pasco's mind had stopped running, frozen around the thought that he would never be allowed out of the house again.

Once his inspection was complete, Gran'ther halted and looked at the cousins who stood on the ground. "How did this come about?" he inquired mildly. "Surely you have not learned to fly, or someone would have mentioned it at supper."

"It's all Pasco's fault!" snapped Vani. He thrashed as if he thought he could swim through the air to claw at his young cousin. "He did this!"

Gran'ther's tufted eyebrows rose. "Did he indeed?"

"I didn't mean it," babbled Pasco. "I — I was scared, and he's going to beat me up again —"

"Beat you up?" Gran'ther looked at Vani and then at Pasco. "Again?"

"He's lying to get himself out of trouble," growled Vani, but the girls were shaking their heads.

"He's beaten Pasco before," Gran'ther repeated, to confirm it.

"Yes, sir," replied Haiday, shamefaced.

"And you, future harriers all, you said nothing? You allowed him to do it?" Gran'ther asked it as if he were simply confirming a report. Now all of the cousins but Vani and Pasco nodded, staring at their feet.

"Well," the old man said at last. "Once we have solved the matter at hand, we must talk about this. We cannot turn a bully harrier loose on the people of Summersea. They deserve better care." To Pasco he said, "Can you bring them down?"

Pasco looked at the three captives. Raising, then lowering his arms, he tried to feel magical. Nothing happened. He then hummed the tune, and raised and lowered his arms. That didn't work, either. He was afraid to try dancing — he'd probably just make it worse.

"There's — I have to . . ." he stammered. Gran'ther scowled, and Pasco tried to get his voice under control. "There's someone I need to get," he said. "She — she knows what's wrong with me." If she'll come, he thought, shivering. What if she refused?

"Then fetch her at once," Gran'ther ordered.

Pasco hesitated. "I have to go a ways. I'll be a while."

Gran'ther sat on a bench, folding his hands over the grip on his cane. "No one's going anywhere." When

Pasco still hesitated, the old man's heavy brows snapped together. "*Now,* boy!" he said sharply.

Pasco fled.

It was late when Sandry had returned the night before, and fretting over Pasco had kept her awake long after midnight. As a result, when she woke in the morning, it was nearly ten. She dressed hurriedly and went in search of the duke. She found him in the workroom with Baron Erdogun.

"Uncle, I'm sorry about last night," she said, kissing his cheek before she took a chair. "I had to talk to Lark. I didn't get home until late. And why didn't you wake me for your ride this morning?"

"I am aware you came back late, and before you scold, I heard it this morning. I was abed when you returned." He smiled at her and offered her a plate of muffins. The baron yanked the bell pull. "When you didn't come this morning, I assumed you were still asleep," the duke continued. "Since you're usually up early, I thought you must need your rest. As for my ride, instead of having to make excuses to my taskmaster" — he reached over and tugged one of her braids, which she had left hanging down her back that morning — "I confined my explorations to the Arsenal."

A servant arrived and took breakfast instructions

from Erdogun while Sandry grinned at the duke. The Arsenal dockyards — where Emelan's navy was built, housed, and repaired — was large, but it was nearby. A visit there would not have lasted as long as their ride of the previous morning had.

He *must* have been tired, to go to bed early and to stick to the Arsenal today, she thought, breaking up a muffin. So he's listening to the healers after all, maybe.

"I trust you found Dedicate Lark in good spirits?" asked Erdogun.

Sandry nodded, her mouth full. When she finished her first muffin, she began on her second. Looking up as she buttered it, she saw that both men were watching her. It seemed they were curious about what had taken her up to Winding Circle, but they were too polite to ask her outright.

She giggled, then told them about the success of Pasco's net-spell, and Lark's advice. As she talked, servants brought in a small table and set her breakfast out on it. Once they were gone, she continued as she ate.

When she finished, the duke chuckled. "I'm sure teaching will be an eye-opening experience," he said, picking up the sheaf of papers he'd been reading when she came in. "It always was for me."

"Oh, splendid," Sandry told him drily. "Was there any news about Jamar Rokat?"

"Not a word," said the duke. "It's as if they appeared

in that room, did their work, then vanished." He leafed through the papers until he found three, and passed them to her. Sandry read them quickly. Captain Qais was as stiff in writing as he was in person, but the facts were clear. So far the bodyguards refused to admit to helping the killers enter the countinghouse. She understood that: if they did, they would be executed as accomplices. The Provost's Mages were still picking apart the spells of protection and detection on Rokat House, with nothing to report. Everyone who worked in the building was being questioned by the Guard. The dead man's brother was making a nuisance of himself, hovering over Captain Qais and demanding results.

Sandry returned the papers to her uncle, and continued to eat her breakfast in thoughtful silence. Just as she finished, a maidservant came to the open door. "Forgive me, your grace, my lord, but there is a boy here." In her mouth the word *boy* sounded like a disease. "He says he must speak to my lady immediately."

Sandry frowned. Could it be Pasco? "Does he have a name?" she asked.

Pasco darted in past the servant, coming to an abrupt halt when he saw the two men at the table. His face, already ashy, went dead white.

Sandry took pity on him and got to her feet. "Pasco, good morning," she said calmly, putting her napkin on her chair. "You met my uncle yesterday, of course —"

Pasco bowed jerkily to the duke.

"And this is the Lord Seneschal, Baron Erdogun fer Baigh."

Pasco gave the same wooden-puppet bow to Erdogun, then fixed pleading eyes on Sandry. "Lady, my cousins are hanging in midair and I can't get them down!"

Sandry heard the duke smother a chuckle. She ignored it as she fixed Pasco with her best teacherly stare. "I take it you danced them up there?"

Pasco nodded, wringing his hands.

"So you agree you have magic," Sandry told him sternly.

"I'll agree anything, lady, if only you'll fetch them down!"

Sandry looked at the maid. "Please inform Oama and Kwaben that I require their company, my own horse, and a mount for Pasco." The woman dipped Sandry a curtsy and left, her back stiff with disapproval.

Sandry thrust Pasco into a chair and put a muffin in his hands. "Tell me *exactly* what happened," she ordered.

House Acalon was not what Sandry had thought it would be when Pasco told her that four families of harriers lived there. She had expected something gloomier than this tall, airy building with its tiled roof and plastered walls, built around a large central courtyard. Bright, colorful hangings decorated the walls inside and soft carpets lay underfoot. The walls had been white-washed recently; wooden furniture gleamed under coats of wax. It wasn't cold enough yet for a hearth fire in the front parlor where Pasco led her, but a brazier took the chill off the room and released a whiff of sandalwood to perfume the air.

When they entered the front parlor, a woman got up from a chair next to the brazier, closing the book she had been reading. She was tall and strong-looking, with direct brown eyes and a firm jaw. When Pasco saw her, he gulped audibly.

"Mama," he said, looking down.

"I am Sandrilene fa Toren." Sandry offered a hand to the woman, who grasped it lightly, bowed — she wore loose breeches — and released it.

"Zahra Acalon," the woman replied. "I understand my son has been keeping a few things from us."

Sandry gave Zahra her best smile. "Don't blame him," she said, resting a hand on Pasco's shoulder. The boy quivered like a nervous horse. "I only told him yesterday he had dancing magic. I can't scold him for not believing me. My teacher, Dedicate Lark at Winding Circle, has never heard of dance magic the way he does it."

She wasn't sure, but she thought Zahra softened a little. "He should have told us," she said gruffly. Looking at Pasco she added very firmly, *"Immediately."*

"It's not harrier stuff," muttered Pasco.

Zahra looked rueful. "It's true, my lady," she confessed to Sandry. "Most of what gets talked of here is harrier business — Provost's Guard," she explained.

Sandry nodded. "I understand. When I lived at Discipline, almost all we talked about was magic." It wasn't quite true, but it might help mother and son to relax, if she didn't act critical. "Now, perhaps we should get to the problem. Once we've sorted that out, we can talk about Pasco's education."

"This way," said Zahra, leading them through the house. They walked into a gallery around the inner courtyard. From there Sandry could see the airborne captives, three young people in their teens, all in breeches and shirts, each holding a padded baton. They seemed to be practicing a defense against two attackers on the open ground. Watching them intently from a bench near the low fountain at the center of the courtyard was a tall, slender old man with gray hair combed straight back, a long, straight nose and heavy brows.

He thumped the ground with his cane. "No, no, Reha! You're leaving yourself open for a side attack! Pay attention!"

Sandry ducked her head to keep anyone from seeing her grin. She felt a prickle of respect for Pasco. By her reckoning from his story, his cousins had been in the air for at least ninety minutes. He must have been really determined when he danced them up there, she thought.

Zahra stepped forward. "Excuse me, Gran'ther," she announced. "Lady Sandrilene fa Toren has come to help Pasco unravel this" — she glanced at the hanging trio — "difficulty."

The Acalons turned and bowed to Sandry. Even the three in the air tried to bow. This time she'd thought ahead; she raised her handkerchief to her nose to hide her grin at the sight of those three swaying bows.

The old man shot a look at Pasco. "Was there no one of our own standing you could bother with this?" he demanded sharply. "I am sure my lady is far too busy to undo your tangles."

Sandry curtsied to the man Zahra had called "Gran'ther." "Actually, I'm honored to be the mage who discovered Pasco's talent," she remarked solemnly. "Not everyone gets to find unusual magics." Perhaps a white lie on her part would make Pasco feel better, and get his family to think of this as an opportunity, not an embarrassment. "I look forward to being his teacher."

"Teacher!" barked the old man. "Since when does the nobility teach?"

"My lady, this is my husband's father, Edoar Acalon," Zahra said quietly. "He is the head of our house."

Sandry walked over to the three who hung in the air. Halting beside the old man she answered him. "Since the nobility is the mage who discovered his talent, and there are no dance-mages at Winding Circle."

With a nod, she turned her back on Edoar Acalon, making it impossible for him to argue with her. Focusing on the captives, Sandry walked around them, thinking hard.

"I don't think I've seen anything like this before," she remarked slowly. She had Pasco's measure by now. He was capable of forgetting his scare the moment his cousins were earthbound again. She had to reinforce his fright, or he would be skipping lessons before she could say "Duke's Citadel." "None of us ever hung anyone in midair."

Pasco gulped: she could hear him. "You can't fix it?" he cried. "But you have to! I don't know how to get them down!"

She wanted to take pity on him, but something warned her not to let him relax just yet. It's not what I would have chosen for his first lesson, she admitted to herself, but it's what we have — and maybe it'll stick longer this way.

Sandry shook out her skirts, letting Pasco stew a little more. His mother Zahra stood at parade rest, her eyes never leaving Sandry's face, while the old man leaned on his cane.

"If you didn't know how to get them down, you shouldn't have put them up there," Sandry remarked at last.

"It was an accident!" cried Pasco. "I told you how it happened!"

"It's all right if you don't know you're a mage," a girl pointed out.

"Don't help, Reha," muttered Pasco.

"But he does know," replied Zahra woodenly. "Lady Sandrilene told him. He was supposed to tell us, and take lessons with her."

"Of course he knew," Sandry added, her voice cool. "You had to dance, didn't you? You had to think of a tune and hum."

"I want him arrested!" cried Vani, pointing at Pasco. "He knows magic and he did it to me, and that's against the law! I want him harried!"

"You will be silent, Vanido Acalon." Gran'ther Edoar's voice was splinters of ice. "You have said more than enough today."

"Please get them down," Pasco begged Sandry. "I'll do whatever you say. I'll take lessons, whatever you want. *Please.*"

Sandry looked at Zahra. "Have you a private room we can use?" she asked.

The woman nodded, and led them back into the house. Sandry followed, towing Pasco. When Zahra showed them into a small chamber just off the gallery, Sandry thanked her and closed the door.

"Sit," she ordered Pasco. "Take some deep breaths. It's just you and me here. Calm down."

Pasco nodded and sat on the floor, inhaling and exhaling loudly. Sandry looked around. From the scent of incense and the statues of gods in wall-niches, she guessed they were in the family chapel. She recognized most of the gods: Lark's own patroness, Mila of the Grain, the earth goddess, and her consort the Green Man; Yanna Healtouch, the goddess of water and health; Shurri Firesword, the goddess of fire and warriors; and Hakkoi the smith, god of forges and the law. She paused before the only unfamiliar statue: a man with a hawk's head, feet, and wings in brown and blue feathers, and a long black coat. A sword and dagger hung from the belt at his waist. In one hand he carried a lantern, in the other a set of manacles. From the number of votive candles and half-burned sticks of incense around the niche, he seemed to be very popular in this household.

"That's Harrier the Clawed," Pasco informed her. His voice was steadier. "The god of provosts, guards, and thief-takers. He takes apart secrets and puts them away against the starving time. There're shrines to him in every coop — every guardhouse. And here."

Sandry turned to look at Pasco. "First things first," she said. "You need to learn to meditate. Or at least, you need to be able to clear your mind if you're handling magic. Now's as good a time as any to start."

"But Vani and them," he objected.

"They've been up this long, a bit longer won't hurt," Sandry replied firmly.

Pasco rubbed his face with hands that trembled. "Why did this happen?" he whispered. "All I want is to dance. Not to be a mage, no, nor a harrier neither. Just a dancer. Now I can't even do that without something going awry."

"The quicker you learn to control your magic, the sooner you can dance and not worry," she pointed out. "So calm down, and we'll start." He swallowed hard and nodded, looking at his hands.

She was about to teach him the proper way to breathe when she realized that *she* had almost forgotten something very important. "I need to ward us," she said tersely, silently cursing herself. How could she not remember that meditation with an untrained mage would cause his magic to spill all over? Her teachers had been careful to ward her and her friends when they first began their studies.

She dragged her red thread from her belt purse. I'm not ready to teach anyone, she thought as she pulled away the loose end. What else am I going to forget?

"What's a ward?" asked the boy.

"It's like a fence that keeps magic in. Or other things out, if that's what you set your wards against. Now hush." Sandry thrust her irritation with herself out of her mind and began to lay her thread down in a circle that would enclose both her and Pasco. Once it was complete and she had stepped inside, it took but a touch of power to break the thread from the spool, then join the ends to close her circle. Shutting her eyes, she raised her power until it formed a bowl that enclosed them completely.

Once that was done, she settled on the floor next to Pasco, arranging her skirts. "Until you control your power, meditation will make it spill all over," she told him. "Don't meditate without an older mage present until I say you can."

"Oh, splendid," he grumbled. "Another thing I can't do now without a nursemaid."

Sandry shook her head. If he was in the glooms, nothing she could say would improve his mood. It was better to get on with the lesson.

As if he could hear Sandry's thoughts, the boy grinned sheepishly. "You're more patient than Mama, lady. She would've smacked my head by now, and told me to" — he stopped. What his mother would have said was probably too vulgar for the lady — "to quit being a chufflebrain."

Sandry giggled. "Chufflebrain — my friend Briar says that. Now. On to serious matters. Close your eyes, and don't think about anything but what I tell you."

She taught him how to breathe: inhale to a count of

seven, hold for a count of seven, exhale to the same count. Getting him to empty his mind was another matter. He shifted on his haunches; his fingers tapped out a drumroll before she stopped him. From the way his eyes shuttled behind his lids, he was thinking of something with movement to it — not what she wanted.

When she sensed that his body at least was more relaxed than it had been when they started, she said, "Now, think a moment. How can you undo what you've done out there?"

He looked at her, startled. "'Undo'? Why — that means doing what I did, only backward."

She smiled at him. "It does, doesn't it?" Reaching over, she touched her thread circle. It broke; she felt the power in her ward draining back into her. A nudge of her finger, and the thread rolled itself up. She then reattached it to the spool in her belt-purse. Glancing up, she saw that Pasco was staring at her. "Surely you knew I was a stitch witch," she remarked, amused by his wondering look.

"I heard you was more than that," he said, scrambling to his feet. He offered her a hand. She took it, and let him pull her to her feet. "I never thought you'd fuss with plain old thread."

She led the way out. "Thread's as important to my magic as dance steps will be to yours," she told him as they emerged into the courtyard gallery.

"— why the gods gifted a flibbertigibbet like my grandson with magic," Edoar Acalon was telling Zahra, who was seated beside him.

The girl Reha made a shushing noise and flapped a hand wildly at Sandry and Pasco. Sandry shook her head. It seemed there were reasons why her new student thought that nothing he did mattered.

"Oh, look, it's tippy-feet, *finally*," Vani cried. "You'd better get me down from here, Pasco!"

Sandry halted before the three airborne Acalons, eyeing Vani as if he were a bug she might swat. "What did you do to reach this point?" she asked Pasco.

He moved to a spot three yards in front of the captives. "I did a triple step left and a triple step right," he said, half to himself, half to her. "I was humming music. And then I did that beautiful swan leap the Capchen dancers were practicing —"

"I knew it!" shouted Vani. "You were ogling dancers while *I* did the work —"

Sandry had heard enough. She pointed at him and ordered, "Be silent," putting a twist of her power into it. Vani's mouth snapped shut. Everyone could hear sounds in his throat; he fought to move his jaws, but he could not open his mouth. "A swan jump?" Sandry asked Pasco. "A jump goes up. Aren't your cousins up enough already?"

"He should jump *down*," offered the dangling girl, interested in spite of everything.

"Haiday, shush," said Zahra.

"If you think about the results *before* you try something, you can save yourself problems," Sandry told Pasco. "It sounds like you really need to look before you leap."

"Jump down, jump down," Pasco muttered, turning to view the courtyard.

Sandry could tell when he realized the benches were too short, and followed his eyes as they rested on the gallery wall. Its waist-high top was the same height as his cousins' dangling feet. Pasco ran over and climbed onto it. "I do the steps, and the humming, and I jump *down*," he said triumphantly.

"And while the ones in the air touch the ground, what happens to those of us who are on the ground already?" Sandry inquired, thinking, Maybe he has some brains after all.

Reha and her sister ran into the gallery. Pasco's mother and grandfather stayed where they were, their eyes calmly on him.

"What do you do when you aren't sure you can control magic?" asked Sandry patiently. He'd never work things out if she fed him the right answers. Of course, that meant she had to think of the right kinds of questions, those that would lead him to the answers. "What if you don't want the power getting away from where you wield it?"

"But —" Pasco began to protest. He went quiet. Sandry waited, hoping this meant that he'd learned he shouldn't argue, but use his head.

It seemed she was right. Pasco closed his eyes and inhaled, counting, and held, counting, and let go, counting. Twice more and his lips began to move as he talked silently to himself.

Then he opened his eyes. "I don't know how to, to put that warding thing on, that you do with the string," he pointed out. "Do I have to learn now?"

Sandry grinned at him. "It would take you weeks to learn how to do a proper warding," she said. "Only think how inconvenient for your cousins if they were up there all that time. When you need a spell you can't do, it's a good idea to ask an older mage to help. Specifically, you had better ask your teacher."

Pasco bowed his head. "Lady Sandry, please will you ward them?" her asked.

She drew her red thread from her belt-purse. "Stay right there. I have to include you in the ward." He obeyed, holding his position atop the gallery wall, as relaxed as if he stood on solid ground.

Here there was no way she could lay her thread flat as she had when they meditated. Instead she walked through the gallery and around the captives, letting her thread drape over the low wall. When her circle was complete, she stood back and called on her magic. The scarlet thread rose until it stopped six feet above the ground, at waist level on the cousins in the air. Sandry let her power surge, enclosing her, Pasco, and the captives in an unseen bubble. Everyone else was outside.

"Now, Pasco," she told him quietly.

He took a deep breath, then began to hum. Nimbly he danced three quick steps left and three more right, then leaped. It seemed as if he floated to the ground, touching as lightly as a feather on the ball of one foot.

Vani and the girls did not land that gently. They dropped.

Pasco faced Sandry. "It worked!" he cried, giddy with excitement. "We did it!"

She plucked at her thread. It broke, still hanging in midair, and she wound it onto her fingers. "That's what happens when you think it through," she told him. "Now, let's go talk about lessons." She, Pasco, and Zahra had reached the door to their part of the house when Gran'ther thumped his cane imperiously on the court-yard tiles. They turned. Vani was clawing at his mouth, trying to get it open.

"He really shouldn't be left that way, my lady," Zahra murmured.

Sandry shrugged, and snapped her fingers. Vani's

mouth flew open. He lunged forward, bent on mischief, only to fall flat on his face. Gran'ther had reached out with the head of his walking stick to trip him. "You will come with me," he told Vani, getting to his feet. "I have several things to say to you, and to your parents."

Sandry curtsied to the old man, then walked into the house with Pasco and his mother. "We need to set a time and place for Pasco's next lesson," she told Zahra. "I think he's seen that he really needs to study."

Alzena raced up the rickety steps of the inn and pounded at the door to their room. She could hear Nurhar scramble to open it.

"Be more careful," Nurhar told her once she was inside. "What if you draw attention?"

"Two roughs are trying to cut each other to pieces downstairs," she snapped at him. "They wouldn't notice aught else if the place was on fire." She turned to the mage. "The brother, Qasam Rokat. He's come out of his Silk Place house. We can take him easily when he returns." Her grin bared long, yellow teeth. "He is sweating."

The mage looked up at her. There was an emptiness in his eyes that gave her the jitters. "Is there salt for me?"

"No," she said cruelly. The dragonsalt they fed him kept him dreamy for most of the time. "It's time for you to wake up and earn your next dose."

"Yes," he replied. "But a taste will clear my mind."

"Work first," she told him, sharp-voiced. "When we have Qasam Rokat's head, then you can have salt."

He had not blinked. That made her uneasy. "I have to see the place."

"We know that," she snapped.

"I don't like it," mumbled Nurhar as he positioned the carry-frame on the rickety bed. "It's too public." He lifted the mage into the frame. There was so little of him — he had no legs and his body was skeleton-thin from his long use of dragonsalt — that Alzena could pick up the mage at need.

"It has to be public," Alzena retorted, fastening the buckles that held the mage to the left side of the frame as Nurhar did the right. "The Rokats have to know that nothing will stop us."

Once the mage was settled, Alzena and Nurhar dressed in beggars' rags. They covered their clothes and their curved swords with long, patched cloaks that could be stowed in a carry-sack once they were clear of the inn. There was no sense in allowing the locals to wonder how three beggars could afford to rent rooms — even at a pit like this.

Once Nurhar had settled his cloak, Alzena helped him to strap the carry-frame on his back. "All ready for a stroll, Grandpa?" she asked the mage.

"I'm ready to die," he whispered. "I'll be readier still in an hour."

"Too bad," Alzena told him.

"I need dragonsalt."

"Shut up," Nurhar growled, opening the door.

"Help us kill the rest of our prey, and you'll have more dragonsalt than you know what to do with," Alzena hissed in the mage's ear as she followed him and her husband out of the room.

"Sure I will," the mage whispered. He stared blankly at the filthy ceiling as they descended the stairs.

The duke stared at the card the footman had brought. His nostrils flared with distaste. "He will not set a proper time?"

"Your grace, he said it was important."

"His brother's murder, doubtless. Show him in." As the footman left them, the duke told Sandry and Baron Erdogun, "It is Qasam Rokat — Jamar Rokat's brother. No doubt he feels not enough is being done." Sandry and the baron rose, but Vedris shook his head. "Please stay. This is a complex affair — perhaps you will see what I do not. I should leave this to the provost and her people, but it is my sense that the more heads are put to this thing, the better. Is there any way to reach Niko?" he asked Sandry.

The girl shook her head. Tris's teacher, Niklaren Goldeye, was not just the greatest living truthsayer, able to spot a lie at a glance; he was one of the few who could work the magic that made it possible to see the past, even if only for a short time. "They're halfway between here and the Cape of Grief," she said, naming the southern-most tip of land below the Pebbled Sea. "That's much too far away. I won't even be able to talk to Tris until they return to Hatar."

"And that will be?" inquired Erdogun.

"Not till next year." She sighed.

The duke smiled. "You miss her, don't you?"

"I miss them all," Sandry admitted. "It's like part of me left with them. At least I can still mind-speak to Daja and Briar, if I really strain."

The duke reached over to pat her hand. "Well, I am delighted you stayed at Winding Circle."

The door opened. Sandry had been present at such meetings before and kept her workbox here for them. Quickly she lifted her embroidery hoop from the box and began to stitch on its design. She was the very picture of a noble maiden.

"Qasam Rokat, of Rokat House, merchants," the footman announced before he closed the door behind the guest. Sandry peered under her lashes at the new-comer. Qasam Rokat was plump, not fat like his brother had been. He was sweating so much that his white tur-ban had gone dark where the lower edge touched his skin. His face was brown, his full dark beard neatly trimmed. Like Jamar Rokat, he was richly clothed in silk, wearing draped breeches under a long, buttoned coat. The sword and knife sheaths at his sash were empty — the Guards would have taken his weapons before allowing him to come before the duke. He repeatedly dabbed his forehead and cheeks with a silk handkerchief.

First he bowed to the duke, touching his forehead, then his chest, with both hands as the people of Aliput greeted their royalty. When he straightened, he bowed less formally to Baron Erdogun.

When he noticed Sandry, he frowned. "Your grace, what I have to say is not for a lady's ears."

"Lady Sandrilene has my confidence," replied the duke coldly. "I value her advice. Moreover, she is an accomplished mage with a broad education. You may speak before her and the baron as you would privately to me."

"But your grace," argued the man, bowing once more to Sandry, "it regards matters of considerable violence and bloodshed. Surely you do not wish so lovely a young lady —"

"Either talk or go away," snapped the baron. "It is not for you to question his grace."

The duke raised a hand. "Peace Erdo." To Qasam Rokat he said, "My caretakers are zealous. Speak before them or not at all."

Sandry felt the merchant's eyes on her. She kept hers down, picking out a design of blue lotuses, their petals and stems shaping the signs for health. It was complex work; most embroiderers would be able to attend to nothing else while they stitched.

"Your grace, I appreciate your seeing me at such a time," Qasam said at last. "My deepest felicitations on your recovery, so prayed for —"

Again the duke raised his hand. "Spare me your felicitations and prayers. If you have concerns about your brother's murder, why have you not addressed them to my lady provost? The investigation is her affair, not mine."

"But your grace understands the way of the world," Qasam replied. "A servant always works better when the master's eye is upon him. I wished to assure myself that your grace's eye is indeed upon my lady provost and her guards. It is known that your grace is not a — a supporter of Rokat House."

The duke braced his elbows on his chair and folded his hands. "Let us speak frankly," he said in an icy voice. Hairs stirred on the back of Sandry's neck. Suddenly he looked — he *felt* — dangerous. "I permitted your house to do business here under certain conditions. The thievery and murder you employ were never to occur in Emelan, or you would be barred from my lands, and I would find other ways to obtain myrrh. Is that not so?"

Qasam bowed. He was trembling now as well as sweating.

"From where I sit, it appears that your methods outside my borders have come within them. What act did the Rokats commit to rate your brother so messy an execution? And if you think to retaliate, you and your people are on the next ship out."

"No, your grace, please! We did nothing to cause this, nothing!"

"I find that hard to believe," drawled Erdogun.

Qasam threw him a frantic look, then dropped to his knees before the duke. "Please, you must help us! We have done nothing in Emelan, on my mother's honor I swear it! The Dihanur are animals, my poor brother is evidence of that —"

"Now we come to it. Get up," the duke said crossly. "Don't grovel." He glanced at the baron, who tugged the bell pull.

Sandry put aside her embroidery and got a chair for Rokat. The man struggled to his feet and sagged into the chair, weeping. She watched him for a moment, then lifted his handkerchief from his fingers.

"As a rule, silk isn't practical for handkerchiefs," she told him. "It's expensive and it looks nice, but it doesn't soak up moisture very well." She gave hers to him, and laid the silk over the back of his chair to dry. Qasam rolled his eyes at her — they were bloodshot from weeping and fear — and buried his face in the new handkerchief.

A soft-footed maid brought glasses, a bottle of wine,

and a bottle of pomegranate juice. Sandry poured wine for the men and gave out the glasses, then took some juice for herself. Mages soon learned that any drug or liquor had unusual effects on their power, some good, many bad. She didn't think Qasam Rokat would like it if all the threads in the room began to move.

His sips of wine seemed to quiet the merchant. "Thank you, your grace," he whispered.

"I do not require thanks. You suspect your rivals the Dihanur are involved?"

Qasam nodded. "I know it."

"Have you favored my lady provost with this information?"

Qasam shook his head.

"Why not?" asked the duke.

Qasam did not look up. "My lady — she, she is not a woman of power, in the merchant's world, or, or understanding, or sympathy."

"His grace knew that when he asked her to take the post," said Erdogun waspishly.

Sandry, back at her embroidery, was fascinated. She had to suppose that the baron and the duke had done this many times. She knew her great-uncle; if the baron made tart observations in situations like this, it was because the duke wanted him to.

They stir the pot, and see what bubbles to the top, she thought.

"The provost thinks it is not a business matter, when murder is done with such violence," Qasam explained, staring at the glass in his hands. "She expects a slighted husband or lover, or a madman." He began to tremble again. "She does not understand the Dihanur. They are heartless, little better than animals —"

"You said that," the baron interrupted. "Tell us something new."

Now Qasam did look up. His skin gleamed with sweat. "We are rivals. They have the frankincense trade and desire our monopoly on myrrh as well, the greedy pigs. And somehow they have learned, they found —" He drained his glass and set it down, shaking so hard that he nearly dropped it. "Today I received word they have gained the upper hand. In Bihan, in Janaal. My — my father is dead, my mother, their parents, my sisters, and their husbands . . ." He covered his face with his hands.

"You believe your brother's killing was part of this." Duke Vedris made it a statement, not a question.

Qasam lowered his hands. "They mean to wipe our house from the world. In Bihan, in Janaal, they have succeeded. Now they send their murderers here. My brother Jamar was the first — they will not stop until they have killed every Rokat in Emelan."

The duke got to his feet; the baron and Qasam did the same. Sandry began to rise, but the duke shook his head at her.

"They shall commit no mass slaughter here," Vedris told Qasam. "Tell all this to my lady provost and her harriers — they will find it useful. You may have obstructed their search by keeping information back. And think of the rest of your family in Emelan — they will need protection."

"Don't bunch up in one building," said Erdogun. "You don't want to make it easy for them."

Qasam nodded. He was spent with emotion; Sandry wondered if he'd slept at all last night.

"I am curious," the duke remarked, standing idly at rest. "Were you told how your brother was found?"

The merchant nodded, wiping his face again.

"Murderers rarely stop to arrange their work. The way they left things suggests" — Vedris paused, searching for the right word, while his eyes never left Qasam's drooping form — "it suggests a message. Particularly the display of your brother's head. Am I correct? Was a message intended?"

"It refers to a thing that, that was done," whispered Qasam. "My brother in Janaal is — was — intemperate. A Dihanur thrust ahead of our great-uncle as they went into the temple of Tirpu. The insult was avenged on Palaq Dihanur, their patriarch. Then my brother showed all the city what became of those who did not treat the elders of Rokat House with the proper respect."

"He displayed the head —?" prodded the baron.

"On the city walls. Over the south gate, for all to see."

"And you wonder why they're angry," Baron Erdogun growled, disgusted.

Qasam shook his head and looked at the duke. "You will help? Please, I am not . . . My brothers, my uncles, my father, all have spilled blood to defend our house. I am only a bookkeeper, they do not even listen to me. Please say we are under your protection."

"Everyone in Emelan is under my protection," the duke said evenly. "Be sure you inform my lady provost that I suggested you explain these further details to her."

Qasam bowed, touching his forehead and chest. Sandry looked at her uncle reproachfully. Did he really mean to send this poor man back to the city without guards? Qasam would have his own guards, under the circumstances, but the presence of the Duke's Guard would *show* he was under her uncle's eye. The duke glanced at her. His mouth twitched.

"Erdo, go with Master Rokat. Detail a pair of guards to accompany him to my lady provost."

"I must stop at home." Qasam's face was suddenly brighter. "For papers . . ."

"Yes, very well," said the duke. "My guards will stay with you."

Erdogun's bow conveyed respect mingled with re-proach that the duke would bother to give this man extra protection. "By your command, your grace," he said coolly, and ushered their guest out the door.

Alzena waited across the street from Qasam Rokat's home, her curved sword balanced on her knees. She was clad in the essence of nothingness, like her husband Nurhar, and the mage, who was tucked in a niche in a nearby wall. The nothingness was the mage's special power, the unmagic that got them past the cleverest guards and the most powerful spells. It cloaked her and Nurhar and even himself in sheer emptiness. Guards and magical protections felt nothing because nothing was there. She could not even see Nurhar or the mage as she peered through the tiny slit in the spells that enabled her to look at the real world. Late at night she sometimes wondered how it would feel, if that slit were to close. Would the nothingness eat her, as it seemed to have eaten the mage?

What ate him is dragonsalt, her practical self scolded. Keep your mind on the task!

Here came Rokat. She stirred. She had expected his own guards, two in front and two behind. The surprise was that somehow he'd talked Duke Vedris out of a pair of soldiers. They will do him as much good as his own bodyguards, she thought, getting to her feet.

She couldn't see Nurhar, but she knew he had gone to work when the confusion balls burst. They had two for the bodyguards ahead of Rokat, and two for those bodyguards behind him. The guards reeled; their horses staggered as the enclosed drug went into sensitive noses. The balls were good for three minutes, and they hadn't brought extras to cover the duke's men. She would just have to be quick, quicker than the soldiers — but that was why the family had honored her with the task.

As silent as a shark streaking toward prey, Alzena Dihanur ran across the cobblestones, between the lurching horses. The two Duke's Guards closed in around the sweating Rokat, their weapons drawn. Down went the Guardsman's horse on Rokat's left, blood pouring from two hacked legs. That would be Nurhar. He knew if he crippled the mount the rider would be too busy to interfere. Alzena dodged to that side as horse and man toppled away from her target. Sweeping her curved blade up, she sliced through Rokat's saddle girth, not caring that the razor edge bit deep into his animal's side. Grabbing Rokat's clothes, she yanked.

Down he tumbled, screaming, as the other Guardsman tried to shove past the flailing bodyguards to reach him. Alzena hacked Rokat across the belly and thighs, then got into position for her third cut, and made it. Gripping the head by the beard, she thrust it into a bag, spelled like the rest of her with unmagic, and raced down the street with it. She was invincible as long as she bumped into no one; they would never see her, because she was nothing. On she ran, giddy with blood. Nurhar would collect the mage, and return with him to the inn. It was her job to display the head, and she knew just where she would leave it.

The duke's fist struck the mahogany table, making plates and silver jump. "Shurri curse them!" he whispered. "Atop the Market Square fountain, for the world to see!"

Sandry glared at the Provost's Guard who had brought the news. She had just gotten her uncle to sit down to supper when the messenger came with word of Qasam Rokat's murder. Couldn't the servants have kept the woman back until the duke had eaten?

She bowed her head, ashamed of her anger, but a fact was a fact. Qasam Rokat was dead. She'd like to keep her uncle from following him out of life.

"What of the Guardsmen with Rokat?" the duke wanted to know.

"Guryil broke his leg when his mare dropped on him," replied the Provost's Guard. "He's in your infirmary now. His partner, Lebua, is with him. Our people are taking their story."

The duke stood. Sandry got to her feet, fighting to push her heavy chair back.

"My dear," Vedris began, "there is really no need for you to —" He met her eyes and smiled ruefully. "Forgive me. I forgot who I was talking to. I become like poor Rokat, trying to shelter you when you do not want such care." To the messenger he said, "My servants will give you food and a mount for your return. Tell my lady provost I appreciate the prompt notification."

The messenger bowed her thanks.

The walk to the infirmary was a brisk one. Sandry wanted to protest the pace, but the bleak look in her uncle's eyes discouraged her. I can't coddle him forever, she thought as she trotted to keep up. He'll just get impatient and overdo.

Knowing that, it was still hard not to protest. She couldn't forget how he'd looked when, only six weeks ago, she got word that he'd collapsed in his library. When she had reached him, the duke was in bed, his face ash gray and pain-twisted. He looked old and half-dead. It had taken all her strength to bind his spirit to his body until the healers could do their work. She never, *ever* wanted to see him like that again.

As if he felt her worry, the duke slowed near the infirmary door and waited for her to catch up. "I'll be all right," he murmured as a guard opened the door for them. "And I promise I will eat as soon as we're done here."

The injured Guryil lay in a curtained alcove at the rear of the small infirmary. A healer sat with him, one hand on his wrist, the other on a leg braced with splints. To Sandry's magical vision the healer's power was a cool silvery blaze that ran through the Guardsman. It flickered in the broken leg, as if the magic fought something there.

"Guryil has broken that leg several times," remarked a short, stocky man who watched from the curtain's edge. "He's built up a resistance to healing." The speaker was only a handful of inches taller than Sandry, with curly white-and-gray hair cropped short, a salt-and-pepper mustache, and full, dark eyes. He spoke with a crisp Namornese accent, and wore the uniform of the Provost's Guard. His insignia was two yellow concentric circles surrounded by a rayed circle, which meant he was a colonel. The fastenings and trim on his uniform were all white: he was a mage.

"I am told his mount fell," remarked the duke quietly.

"Collapsed, poor beast," the stocky man replied. "Tendons cut in the right fore and hind legs."

"I swear, I saw nothing!" cried the young man beside the bed. He, too, wore the uniform of the Duke's Guards, and he clung desperately to Guryil's free hand. "Not a midget, not a child — Gury's too good to let anyone get close like that, and they didn't use confusion balls on *us*, just Rokat's bodyguards!"

"Confusion balls?" Sandry whispered to the duke.

The stocky man heard and replied, "Clever devices. Mix spells for addlement and visions, throw in a drug to give the horse the staggers, and stitch them in a ball. Throw it at a man's chest, it bursts, and you've got him and his horse useless for three or five minutes, depending." .

"They are illegal," said the duke coldly.

The mage shrugged. "Of course they're illegal — they're for the one purpose, aren't they? More importantly, they cost. Our killers have full moneybags."

The duke went to the Guardsman who sat beside Guryil. "Tell me what happened." He gave a flask to the young man — and where did Uncle get that? wondered Sandry — who opened it and took a long drink.

She squinted at the Guardsman as he returned the duke's flask and began to talk. There was something, not in him but *on* his sleeve, like a brush of ash, something that felt alien. She wanted to go closer to look, but he was far too nervous. His full lips trembled as he talked and his eyes flicked repeatedly to the man on the bed.

"Guryil is the solid partner," the harrier-mage murmured. "Guardsman Lebua is superb with a blade and a quick thinker, but he needs a calm hand on the rein."

Sandry nodded, and took a better look at Guryil. He was brown to Lebua's black, a few years older, with long, crinkled hair mussed from lying on a pillow. The healer seemed to ease his pain if not mend his leg. The lines in Guryil's face were not so sharp, his body more relaxed, than when she arrived.

A shadowy smear lay on Guryil's splinted leg, a long stripe from his thigh to his foot. The healer's magic flickered in the flesh under it, like a candle shining through dirty glass.

"What *is* that?" Sandry whispered, staring.

"What is what?" asked the mage.

"The shadow on his leg. You can see the healing through it."

"Seeing, is it?" The harrier-mage fumbled at a ribbon around his neck. A glass round set in a copper rim hung from it. He raised it to one eye and walked closer to Guryil, leaning over him.

The healer glared at him. "Do you mind?" he asked. "This is hard enough without *you* meddling."

The mage returned to Sandry. "It's a shadow, all right," he said, tapping his palm with the glass. Sandry glanced at it, and caught the glint of vision-spells written into lens and rim. Niko had spelled Tris's spectacles that way four years ago, before first Tris and then the rest of them developed the uncommon ability to see magic on their own.

"Who are you, please?" Sandy asked the mage.

He bowed. "Wulfric Snaptrap at your service, my lady."

"Wulfric pain-in-the-rump," muttered the healer.

"Now, if you'd just let me talk to him —" said Wulfric.

"He was in pain. He's in less pain now, but I want him in *no* pain. Then you can muddle his poor head with questions," replied the healer.

"I wonder . . ." murmured Sandry, thinking aloud. "Could something fight your power? Another magic?"

"Something you may not recognize," Wulfric added. "*I* certainly don't."

The healer glared at them. "If it's a magic I haven't seen before, how would I know if I were fighting it?" he demanded. "I admit, Gury here should be resistant to healing, but not like this. The more I pour in, the less it helps."

Sandry opened her mouth, then closed it. She wasn't sure that either of these men would let her do something.

"Speak up, my dear," the duke said from his seat beside Lebua.

"Master healer, might I try something?" she inquired. The longer she looked at that shadow, the queasier it made her feel. She wanted it off the injured Gury and his partner Lebua as well.

The healer raised his brows. "What did you have in mind, my lady?"

She stepped forward. "Take your magic out of him. All of it." Guryil's eyes flew open. "I'm sorry, Guardsman," Sandry told him, "but I really think this must be done."

Guryil nodded reluctantly.

The healer laid his hands on the broken leg. Sandry watched as all of his magic flowed out of his patient and back into him. Guryil whimpered, and sweat poured off his forehead. His pain had returned.

Sandry rested her hands against his foot, her fingers just missing the shadow. She closed her eyes and fell into the heart of her magic. Swiftly she collected what she needed, sorting her power into a thousand hair-fine strands.

She opened her eyes. Looking through her power, she could see the healer's magic, Wulfric's blaze — accented by bright spots that were the spelled tools he carried — and the glow from the steady-heart charm the duke's healer had made for Vedris. Against all that brightness, the shadow was still just a thin layer of grime.

She spread her fingers on Guryil's foot, and carefully slipped a thread under that layer. The feel of it against her magic made her skin creep. She *had* to get every shred of it.

Once her thread was under the shadow, she let it grow until she saw it emerge from under the darkness at Gury's thigh. She chose more threads, running them under the smear. Once she had a solid layer of vertical strands, she paid out a fresh thread along the bottom of the strip, at right angles to her vertical ones. The new thread became the smear's lower border. She thrust it then, setting it flying in and out among the vertical threads, weaving tight and fast. This was easy; she sometimes thought she'd spent most of the last four years weaving pure magic.

She felt it when her moving thread hit empty air. Now her woven power lay solidly between that shadow and the injured man. She held her left hand over it and called the free end of the thread back to her. It came, folding the magical cloth in half. She looped her thread around it three times, tying the whole into a tight bundle. Only then did she let her thread break.

"Here," Wulfric said. "I carry these in my kit, just in case." He held up a silk bag that gleamed with signs to enclose and protect. "I'd thought to scrape it off, once you showed it to me. I've got a little spatula that might have done the job."

"I was afraid to miss any." Sandry dumped the bundle into his sack, then called all the power that was hers back into herself. It came away clean — she made certain of that. When she nodded to Wulfric, he tied the silk bag shut. "Go ahead," Sandry told the healer.

He was already hovering. Now he sat and poured his power into Gury. The man sighed; his head fell back on his pillow. The healer looked at Sandry, shocked. "I could feel the difference! Nice work, my lady, *very* nice."

Sandry blushed. "There's some of that stuff on his partner, too," she told Wulfric. He nodded, and they went over to Lebua. Gathering the darkness on him went quickly.

As soon as Wulfric had that second piece of shadow in one of his protected bags, he told Sandry and the duke, "I'm off to play with this. I'll let you know what I find." He strode briskly out of the infirmary.

"What an odd man," Sandry remarked, wiping her forehead on her sleeve. The duke frowned, watching her, then offered his arm. Sandry let him walk her out into the cool night air. A gentle mist was falling. When Sandry turned her face up to it, Duke Vedris paused.

"He is the best of the provost's mages," he said, his velvety voice easy on her ears. "He knows more about the spells used to commit and study crime than anyone else alive. If he can't pick apart what you found, then it must be rare indeed. You could do with supper, I think. So could I."

Sandry nodded, and they returned to the duke's residence. She would have to wash her hands before she ate. Maybe a scrubbing would erase the sense that she had touched something dreadful in handling those smears.

The next morning Pasco arrived after breakfast. When Sandry met him in the great entrance hall, the boy had the look of a hunted fawn. "This place is so *big*," he told Sandry, bowing jerkily. "Don't you get lost, my lady? Should I be here?"

She looked him over. Gone were the sandals, breeches, and worn shirt of the last two days — at Zahra Acalon's command, Sandry guessed. Now he was dressed in what had to be his best clothes: neat brown cotton breeches, a spotless yellow linen shirt, and a thigh-length brown coat that he wore unbuttoned. His feet were neatly shod.

"Don't be silly," she informed him. "Yes, you should be here. I *told* you to be here. No, I never get lost. Let's find someplace quiet." She led him upstairs and opened a door to one of the sitting rooms. A pair of maids had rolled up the carpets and were busily scrubbing the floor. They started to get up, but Sandry shook her head at them and closed the door. "By the way, Pasco, you look nice."

"Mama said I couldn't come here in normal clothes," he explained as they walked down the hall. "She even scrubbed me behind the ears, and me twelve years old! Does his grace really need so many rooms?"

Sandry opened another door, to find it was one of the side entrances to the chancellory. Scribes turned to stare at her. She closed the door. "His grace's officials need the rooms," she told Pasco severely. "We'd better go outside." And I had better think of someplace else for us to meet, she realized. Pasco just isn't comfortable here.

A stair led them out into the gardens. They found a seat on a stone bench that was tucked out of the day's brisk wind. Sandry perched crosswise on it and drew her legs up in a tailor's seat under her skirts. She pointed sternly to the bare spot on the bench in front of her. Pasco sat. "Do you remember how we meditate?" she wanted to know.

"You have to ward us," he said, mischief in his eyes.

Sandry drew herself up and got off the bench with great dignity. "So you *do* remember yesterday's lesson, at least a bit." Let him think she had meant it as a test. He didn't need to know that mentally she was yelling at herself for almost forgetting such an important thing.

She had to calm down to place the thread circle and enclose them in her power. By the time she rejoined him on the bench, she had to admit that, since she *did* ward them before his magic could spill, it was funny. Not that she would tell him so, but she thought that the duke might laugh at the tale.

"What next?" she asked.

"I close my eyes and breathe and count and think of nothing," he replied promptly. "Even if I'm bored."

"Very good," she approved. "And today I want you to imagine you're fitting yourself into something small —"

"Like what?"

Sandry tried to remember how Niko had explained it to them. Briar had chosen a carved wooden rose, Sandry a drop spindle, Daja a smith's hammer. Tris had never said what she had imagined. "Well, it could be one of the rocks here —"

"Why ever would I want to fit into a rock?"

"Then maybe something you use at home," Sandry told him, trying to be patient. "A candle holder, or a baton. Anything, as long as it's small. You have to learn to pull all your power within your skin, so it won't escape you."

He remembered the pattern of counting and breathing, which pleased her. Getting him to empty his mind remained a struggle. She had to wonder if she and her friends hadn't *needed* meditation to harness their power. The first time they had tried fitting their minds into something small, they had done it easily. Pasco pretended to try, then complained that it was too hard. He had to scratch; he fidgeted. She called his attention back to meditation. At last, the Citadel's giant clock struck the hour, completely destroying the mood.

Sandry got stiffy to her feet and took up her warding. "Will you at least think of something to fit into?" she asked.

"I'll try, my lady," he told her. His look made her think he might agree, but he wouldn't do it. What would make this exasperating boy learn the things he needed to?

Lark had suggested bribes. Busily Sandry shook out her skirts, driving the wrinkles from the cloth. "Pasco," she said craftily, "the sooner you learn to pull in your magic, the sooner you can dance without surprises. You might want to think about that. And if you learn to control your breathing, you'll be able to dance longer." Guiding him out of the courtyard, she asked, "Do you know Fletcher's Circle?"

He frowned. "Between Spicer Street and Fountain Street, off Bowyer Lane?"

"That's it," Sandry replied as they entered the castle. Fletcher's Circle was closer to East District than to Duke's Citadel; she would have to travel longer to get there, which was just as well. The easier things were for Pasco, the less chance that he would try to skip his lessons. "There's an eating-house —" she began.

"The Crooked Crow," he said promptly as they walked into the front hall.

"Yes. Let's meet there tomorrow at this same hour." That would give her time to ride with her uncle and have breakfast before she had to meet him.

Pasco nodded. "May I go now?"

"Fletcher's Circle — don't keep me waiting," she added. "Yes, go."

He trotted out of the residence, his step light. Sandry ran to the door and called after him, "No dancing!" Pasco, halfway across the courtyard, waved at her and kept going.

She sighed and drooped against the heavy door. I am not a teacher, she told herself for the dozenth time. I am much too young. And it's so *hard!*

"Excuse me, my lady." It was one of the maids. "You've guests. I took the liberty of putting them in the rose sitting room."

Sandry thanked the woman. Who might have come to see her? When she entered the room the maid had spoken of, she found Lark and a stranger.

Lark beamed at her. "Sandry, Lady Sandrilene fa Toren, this is Yazmín Hebet." Yazmín curtsied deeply.

Sandry almost gogled, but caught herself in time: it was unladylike. Instead she returned the curtsy. Yazmín Hebet was the most famous dancer around the Pebbled Sea, where the troupes she belonged to had toured for years. Because she danced in public festivals as well as in the castles of the rich, she was popular with all classes of people. Everyone talked of the great Yazmín, from the clothes she wore to the men she was supposed to be involved with.

"This is an honor," Sandry told her. To Lark she said reproachfully, "I didn't know you were friends with the *dancer* Yazmín. All you ever said was you had a friend with that name."

Lark grinned. "I assumed you knew most of my friends outside the temple are performers."

Yazmín smiled. She was pretty, with a tiny nose, large brown eyes, and a small, pointed chin. A mole on one smooth cheek accented a broad mouth with a full lower lip. She wore her tumbled mass of brown hair pinned up, with artful curls left to frame her face. When she spoke, her voice squeaked a little, as if she'd spent years raising it. "I'm honored," she told Sandry. "Lark's told me so much about you. She says you're the only mage she's ever known who can spin magic."

Sandry blushed. "It was spin magic or die, the first time I tried it," she explained. "I was just lucky I figured out how in time. Please, sit down. What can I do for you?"

"Lark says you have a student who's a dance-mage," replied Yazmín, arranging her skirts as she sat. "He needs a teacher?"

Sandry looked from Lark to Yazmín. Was help for Pasco in sight? "You know a dance-mage?" she asked.

"I've never even *heard* of one," said Yazmín. "I've seen shamans work dance spells, just as Lark has, but that isn't the only way they do their magic."

Sandry told herself she should have known she hadn't gotten that lucky. "Then you can recommend a teacher for his dancing? I'll pay his fees," she assured Yazmín. "I can't teach him myself — I know very few dances, and I'm not any good at them."

Yazmín folded her hands in her lap. They were

covered with designs in henna, Sandry noticed, and henna had been used to put red tones in the dancer's hair. She painted her face, too, using kohl to line her eyes and a red coloring on her mouth.

"Actually, I hoped to teach him myself," Yazmín explained. "You see, I retired this year. I've been a traveling dancer for —"

"Twenty-three years," murmured Lark.

Yazmín wrinkled her nose. "You had to remind me. *I* would have been content with just 'a long time.'"

Sandry giggled, and Yazmín smiled at her. "You aren't like most nobles I've met," she commented. "Lark said you weren't." She leaned forward, resting her elbows on her knees. "This summer I opened a school on Festival Street. It's an old warehouse, not fancy, but it's a place where dancers and acrobats can stay and train during the winter. And I've tried to learn the local dances everywhere I've ever been. Your boy could study with me. Between you, me, and Lark, we can craft the kind of spells your boy could do."

"I think you're the answer to my prayers," replied Sandry with relief. "The longer I know him, the more of a handful he is."

"Tell me," Yazmín ordered.

Sandry did, starting with what she had seen on the beach of the fishing village only two short mornings ago, and going straight on through the foul-up that had set three people hanging in midair. She had finished describing her conversation with Pasco's formidable mother at the end of her visit to House Acalon when the door opened and the duke came in.

"My dear, I heard Dedicate Lark was with you and came to say hello," Vedris explained as they all got to their feet.

Lark bowed slightly — temple dedicates were not expected to show great courtesies to nobility. "It's *very* good to see your grace," she told him with a smile. "You're looking well this morning."

The duke smiled back at her. "The loan of my great-niece has much to do with that, I believe."

"It's good to know she's valued as she ought to be," replied Lark. "Your grace, may I present my friend Yazmín Hebet?"

Yazmín curtsied deeply, so graceful that Sandry was envious: while she could curtsy well, she was always afraid her knees might creak. When the dancer rose, she offered a hand. The duke bowed and kissed it, then released her. "I am a very great admirer of yours," he confessed. "I've seen you dance on many occasions."

Yazmín smiled at him. "I have seen your grace at quite a few of my local performances," she remarked. "I'm honored that I was able to entertain you."

"Shall I have the pleasure of seeing you perform this winter?" asked the duke. "I have been considering opening this place up and entertaining a bit, if Sandry would like to be my hostess."

"Yazmín was just saying that she has retired, Uncle," Sandry pointed out.

"Oh, well, I don't plan to give it all up," protested Yazmín. "Certainly I'd be delighted to dance for your grace."

"Then I must arrange something." Vedris motioned for the women to sit, and took a chair himself. "Dare I hope you're here to advise my niece regarding her new student?"

Sandry explained as Lark and Yazmín added details. The duke had a few suggestions for spells they could try in dances, in part because he had seen much more of Yazmín's repertoire than had Sandry, and in part because he had dealt with mages all his life. Twice Yazmín made him laugh, something that Sandry observed with interest.

When the maid who'd directed Sandry to the room came with a tray of refreshments, she took one look at the gathering and disappeared again. She came back with all that would be needed to serve four instead of three. Once she had set out the food and filled their cups, she left the room. She soon returned, plainly unhappy, curtsied to the duke, and said, "My apologies, your grace, but that mage my lady provost keeps has been worriting the footmen —"

"If you'd just told his grace I was here, I wouldn't have 'worrited' anyone, would I?" inquired Wulfric Snaptrap, coming in on the girl's heels. "I told you I needed his grace and my lady right away." His sharp eyes swept the room and returned to Lark. "Though actually I wouldn't mind getting Dedicate Lark's opinion, either. It's news that should go back to the temple in any case."

Yazmín got to her feet. "Perhaps I should go," she said politely. "My lady, you and your boy can stop by my school whenever you like."

"I see no reason for you to leave, if we may be assured of your discretion," said the duke. "Unless you have pressing errands elsewhere?"

Yazmín resumed her seat. "None, your grace. You have my word that nothing said here will ever be repeated by me." She touched an index finger to her lips and kissed it in promise of silence. The duke smiled.

Sandry raised her eyebrows. Was Yazmín *flirting?* She glanced at Lark, who winked at her. Now, here's an idea, Sandry thought as Wulfric pulled up a chair and the maid left them. Uncle *needs* someone who can make him laugh. Maybe a romance would do him good. It's been years since his wife died. I know he's lonely.

You aren't even sure Yazmín is interested, she told herself.

"Is anyone eating these?" asked Wulfric, eyeing the pastries. The duke told him to help himself and he did.

Soon the maid had returned with another tray and a glass for the provost's mage. Once she was gone, Wulfric looked at the duke and said, "I experimented with the magic Lady Sandrilene took off your Guardsmen. We've a problem and a half. The half is dragonsalt. The mage who cast that dark magic is an addict."

"How do you know that?" Sandry asked, fascinated.

Wulfric smiled. "At Lightsbridge, where harrier-mages train, they teach all manner of spells to detect things. I've only performed the dragonsalt cantrip twice before, but I'd a hunch it might work."

"Wulfric," the duke said, quietly amused, "if we may continue with your report? You and my niece may talk of magical practice another time."

"My report. Oh, right." Wulfric buttered a scone. "Well, if our mage is a dragonsalt addict, it could be his supplier is in Summersea. My lady provost has the street Guards looking for a 'salt peddler. My guess is, whoever brought the mage brought the drug. The locals won't sell it, not with your grace's penalties."

"Dragonsalt is the most vile drug brewed. I won't have it here," the duke said firmly. "You claim a problem and a half, Wulfric. If dragonsalt is the half, what is the whole?"

"We've a mage who deals in —" Wulfric hesitated. "'Unmagic' is the best term. It's — nothingness."

"The absence of all else — of light, magic, existence," Lark said, her eyes troubled. "You're certain, Master Snaptrap?"

"I've been at this for thirty years, Dedicate," Wulfric informed her tartly. "I'm not likely to mistake something that marked."

"My apologies," replied Lark. "It's just so rare . . ."

"You never mentioned it," remarked Sandry, puzzled. "None of you mentioned it to us." She meant herself and her three friends.

"There was no reason to," Lark replied. "None of you showed the least aptitude for it, Mila and Green Man be praised. Unmagic is so rare we never thought you'd encounter it."

"It's a blight as much as magic," Wulfric muttered.

"What can you do with it?" Sandry asked.

"Murder people in plain view, it would seem," remarked the duke, grim-faced. "Walk past human guards and protective spells with no one to suspect you're there."

"People also use it to collapse distances and walk between places, if they can bear it," Lark added. "One man who jumped from Lightsbridge to Nidra through unmagic lay in a fever for a year, raving. Later he wrote that his senses all went dead; he was trapped inside his own mind."

"Can you find who's using it, now that you know what

it is?" inquired Yazmín. "If no one minds my asking," she added when they all looked at her.

"It's not that simple," Wulfric replied.

Lark nodded. "It's an *absence* more than anything. It's hard to track nothing down. I'll bring it before our mage council, but I don't believe there's any way to pick it out, because it isn't really here."

Yazmín shivered. "It sounds like you'd have to be crazy to use it."

"That's the one thing we can be sure of," replied Wulfric. "The poor bleater that's using it *is* going mad. That's the nature of it, don't you see. When you have magic, you have life itself. That's what it's made of. But this nothingness, it's the absence of life, isn't it?"

"The absence of hope, feeling," continued Lark. "The more it's used, the greater its hold on the mage. And if he's taking dragonsalt to manage it, that just makes it worse. The gods help anyone who gets close. His madness will spread, infecting those around him."

"Me, I handle it with gloves and glass instruments," said Wulfric, his eyes bleak. "I don't want it getting under my skin."

Lark got to her feet with a sigh. "You were right, Master Snaptrap, I need to let the mage council know as soon as possible."

She returned to Winding Circle, but the rest of them stayed, and Baron Erdogun joined them. Sandry heard then that those Rokats still in Summersea were being placed under increased guard, one that even killers spelled to be nothing would have to be wary of.

They were getting clever, Alzena thought as she watched the house on Tapestry Lane. It was the home of Fariji Rokat, one of the Rokat House clerks. In their inspection the previous night, she and Nurhar had sensed watchers. Two large beggars dozed near the corner of Yanjing Street, in a neighborhood where servants quickly sent riffraff on their way. The maids who opened the doors and shutters on the houses facing Rokat's were very muscular. They didn't look like civilians at all, but like guards out of uniform. Archers patroled the rooftops along the street. A trip through Cod Alley behind the house showed gardeners and menservants who played dominoes with hands that were blue-knuckled and callused from fighting.

It was to be expected after the first two murders. Alzena and Nurhar had provided for it. This Rokat's protectors were no more imaginative than the Rokat guards in Bihan and Janaal had been.

They had not thought to put more than one disguised guard in front of the stable on Cod Alley that served the Tapestry Lane houses. They had not thought that Nurhar could pass the guard unseen, to leave a small keg of the very flammable jelly called battlefire in the hayloft.

They had not thought that the bunch of rough types —
draymen, coal carriers, and the like — that came roister-
ing down Tapestry Lane now, after a night of spending
Nurhur's coin in a nearby wineshop, might have an argument not far from Rokat's house. Hiring the rough folk
had been the trickiest part: unless watched, they would
drink up their fee before they were needed. Nurhar had
stayed with them until half an hour ago, doling out coins
one at a time, buying food to make sure a few heads
would be clear enough to remember their orders.

Alzena stepped onto a window ledge on Rokat's
neighbor's house. Her target's roof was less than a story
below. Scouting the areas around some of the less
wealthy Rokats' homes had been a task she and Nurhar
had done before they went near Jamar. This location had
been the best; they had saved it for when Duke Vedris
decided to give protection to the Rokat scum. Before
dawn Alzena had walked across roofs to get here, unseen
and unsuspected by the archers, and had entered her current place through the rooftop door. The house's occu-
pants were up and around, but Alzena ignored them.
Her sanctuary was their unused nursery. No one had entered it yet that morning, which saved her the trouble of
killing them. From here it was a four-foot leap to her target's flat roof.

The roughs were a hundred yards away, lurching
closer as they argued.

Peering through the slit in the spells that hid her, Alzena saw a cloud of smoke rise behind the houses. Nurhar's fire arrows had set the Cod Alley stable roof ablaze.

The roughs were fifty yards off. A hamlike fist swung; Alzena heard furious snarls. Two of them waded into each other. Their friends tried to pull them apart, then joined in. Alzena watched. A few house doors opened: those suspicious-looking servants peered out. If they were Provost's Guards in disguise, they would be uneasy. This was a prosperous street. Peacekeepers here moved troublemakers on in a hurry. It would go against their training to stand by during a brawl.

Here came the supposed beggars to watch, maybe to interfere. Now all of the roughs were punching, kicking, wrestling. One of the beggars moved in and went flying. A manservant ran out of a house and dove into the fight, as did the second beggar.

Alzena grinned. Now the other false servants would watch their comrades in the fray — not Rokat's house, or anything that took place three stories overhead.

Hot air patted her; a flat boom sounded from the alley. The keg of battlefire in the burning stable had caught and exploded. Bells pealed and horns called, summoning everyone to fight the blaze. The archers on top of Rokat's house ran to the back of the flat roof.

Alzena checked her rope to make sure it was properly

anchored, then jumped out and across from her window to her target. She landed with a thud that went unheard in the fire alarms' racket. Off with the rope. Walking cat-footed, Alzena reached the door to the house, and eased herself inside. The archers, watching the fire as it tried to jump from the stable to the neighboring buildings, never looked behind them.

Two guards in the garret below had gone to stare out of the tiny dormer window at the fire. Alzena was past them and down the stairs, into the house proper, with no one the wiser.

The family's protectors had moved them to the nursery, the biggest room on the floor below the garret. A nursemaid was playing with the baby in its crib while the young mother spun and told a story to the little girl. Fariji Rokat paced, his dark face tight.

Alzena drew her knife and killed the baby first, one cut, while the maid stared. When she screamed, the mother leaped up so quickly that she knocked over the little girl and the spinning wheel. The mother raced over to see what had become of the infant. Alzena killed the girl-child as she began to cry.

Fariji looked right at them. What did he see? Her knife was spelled with unmagic, like the sword she now drew from the sheath on her back. Rokat wouldn't see the blade, only his little girl as she fell over, bleeding.

He gasped and lunged for the child, just as his wife had gone for the baby. Alzena stepped into his rush and cut at his neck, smiling. He had seen his children die. That was good.

She stuffed his head into her carry-pouch and turned to regard the woman and the maid. They stared at Fariji Rokat's headless body, screaming. Alzena hesitated. Was the woman pregnant again? She was young; they had seemed much in love.

No use taking chances, Alzena thought, and ran the woman through. Going to the side window, she climbed out. Below her was a first-story addition to the house. She dropped onto it with a clatter of tiles.

She felt an arrow's bite. It took her in the calf, punching through the bulge of muscle to the other side. Alzena cursed and rolled off the tile roof. She landed easily on the pile of hay that lay on the ground, waiting for the servants to cover the garden for the winter. More arrows flew around her — the quick-witted archer was shooting fast, trying to hit what he couldn't see. She waited until a man ran out the back door, then slipped into the Rokat house. The real servants had been sent away — only warriors in street clothes were here now, and most of them were running upstairs in answer to the nursemaid's shrieks.

In the room near the front door Alzena stopped to

deal with her injury. First she broke off the arrowhead, then yanked the shaft from her leg. Both went into her carry-pouch with the head; she dared not leave them for any harrier-mages to use. There was some blood, not a lot, and most was going into her boot. If she tried to bandage it here, people would see the bandage apparently floating in midair outside the nothingness spells.

She limped out of the house and into the street. The roughs were still fighting. From the sounds that came from Cod Alley, the fire was out of control. She hobbled down Tapestry Lane, shaking her head.

There ought to be fun in this victory over the hated Rokats. Even the prospect of her family's pleasure in what she did seemed unimportant now. Before coming to the house she had worried about killing the children, but when her work got to that, she had been cold. What was the point to any of this, if she felt nothing?

After lunch, Sandry remembered that she needed some copper beads for a trim on one of her uncle's tunics. Like any noble she could have asked the merchant, whose shop lay on Arrow Road in the eastern part of the city, to send a clerk to her with a selection, but it was too nice a day to stay indoors. The bead merchant, a woman she and Lark dealt with often, was delighted to see her, and had a dozen new types of bead to show her. With a number of packages tucked into her saddlebags, Sandry and her guards turned back toward Duke's Citadel. They decided to cross town on Yanjing Street rather than tangle in the afternoon crowds on streets like Harbor, Gold, and Spicer. They were a block west of Market Square when Kwaben pointed out a billow of smoke ahead, marking a fire. As they rode closer — the blaze was on one of the little streets that emptied onto Yanjing — they began to hear talk. A bunch of drunks brawling had started it, some people argued. Others said that Provost's

Guards were protecting a merchant from assassins, and the killers had started the fire.

Hearing that, Sandry and her guards followed the gossip past the alley where the fire was and onto Tapestry Lane. The Provost's Guards had set wooden barricades there. Inside them a group of tavern roughs sat, faces sullen, roped together as prisoners under three Guards' eyes. Another Guard questioned a young woman in a nursemaid's cap and apron who sat on the steps to a house. She rocked back and forth, weeping, scarlet hands pressed to her face.

The Provost's Guards would have liked to keep Sandry outside the barriers on both ends of the street, but they couldn't refuse a noble who was also a mage. Grudgingly they let her through. Passing the barricade, Sandry glimpsed dark smears on the steps and walkway before the house where the guard questioned the nursemaid. The hairs on the back of her neck prickled.

She dismounted and took her mage's kit out of a saddlebag. Then she backed Russet to the other side of the barrier, blocking Kwaben and Oama when they would have followed. "Stay there," Sandry told them. "There's something I need to see."

"My lady," protested Oama.

Sandry shook her head. "I'll be within view unless I go inside — and there's plenty of provost's folk about, aren't there?" Sandry looked at the female Guard holding the barricade, who nodded. "So inside I'll be safe, too. The fewer people who walk around here, the better. Close up," she ordered the Guard.

The woman swung the barricade into place. "I don't know that you should monkey about here, my lady," she said, eyeing Sandry's kit with mistrust.

"Master Wulfric Snaptrap will vouch for me," Sandry replied, though she wasn't sure of that at all. What she *was* sure of was that those smears of darkness, if they were the same as those on Guryil and Lebua the night before, had to be protected until Snaptrap could look at them himself. Does this stuff rub off on people? she wondered, approaching the Rokat house slowly, inspecting the ground before her and on either side. Would it stick to anyone as it had to Lebua and Gury? She couldn't take a chance on whether it might or might not.

She reached the house without seeing any smears between it and Yanjing Street. "So far, so good," she murmured.

The Guard who spoke to the crying nursemaid turned away from the woman in disgust. He looked at Sandry. "Who let *you* in?" he growled.

"I'm Sandrilene fa Toren, the duke's great-niece," she said, examining the steps for dark smears. A number of them stretched from the door along one side of the steps to disappear under the sobbing woman. Sandry glanced at her and swallowed hard. The woman's hands, which from a distance looked as red as paint or dye could make them, were covered in blood. Her cap, apron, skirt, and blouse were splotched and her shoes nearly black with it.

Sandry took a breath to clear her head of the giddiness of shock, thinking, I have *got* to get smelling salts. To the unhappy Guardsman she said, "Can she move? There are signs of magic here, and she's sitting right on them."

"Of course there's magic," said the Guard bitterly. "Murdering beasts walk by twenty-four of us to hack up four people, two of them kids — you bet there's magic in it." He bent down and gripped the woman by the elbows, lifting her. "Up, wench — you're sitting on magic."

Sandry stared at him. "Two *kids?*" she asked, horrified.

"Two little ones. This girl was their nurse," explained the Guard. "Says they all died in front of her, and she didn't see what done it."

Sandry met his eyes. "She probably didn't," she whispered.

"I know," replied the man, grim-faced. "Story's too stupid to be true, elsewise."

"You'll have to take my word for this," Sandry told him, "but I can see traces of the magic they used to hide themselves. It comes straight down these steps from the house, and goes that way." She pointed down the street. "I'm going to cover it, to protect it, till your harrier-mages can see it."

The Guard raised his eyebrows. "That's right sensible of your ladyship," he said, his manner more respectful than it had been earlier. "Go ahead, do it."

In her kit she normally kept a number of spelled cloth squares she could use to handle things she didn't want to touch with bare skin. She used some on the marks on the steps between the door and the street, then warned the Guards in the house away from the broad streaks she could see on the wall beside the door. They wouldn't let her inside. Sandry accepted that and followed the marks down the street instead, covering each with a cloth square and murmuring the words that would start its protective spell. Anyone about to touch one of those squares would instantly want not to. They'd want to get away from the square and whatever it covered.

She ran out of them where the marks turned onto the walkway. Now what? she thought, looking at the smears: they led straight toward the far barricade. The more she saw, the stronger was her urge to cover them, to protect others from them, but she had never imagined a situation where she'd need more than fifteen of her cloths. She supposed she could send her guards to a cloth merchant. The problem with that was that she would have to wait here idly, while anything might happen to the unprotected marks.

Sandry turned to look at the house, and heard a rustle — her own clothes. Of course! she thought, triumphant. She wore a silk undershirt beneath her blouse and tunic, and long silk breeches under her wide-legged pants. They wouldn't let her in the house to remove her underclothes, but there was no need to go indoors, if she managed things properly.

She spread her magic into her underthings. It only took a breath of time to make everything she wore attuned to her and her power. Within a second breath, she felt material slide as stitches pulled out of seams. Her top slid under her waistband, rolling to form a snake of silk that wriggled down one leg of her breeches and out. Next she undid the stitches in her under-breeches, letting the cloth pull apart into its separate pieces. She felt silk gliding down her legs and bent over. The pieces crawled into her hands, one pant leg at a time. She looked reproachfully at them: the threads that secured her delicate lace to the cloth had refused to give up their treasure.

Now, she told them silently. The threads resisted a moment longer, then glided out of the cloth. The lace bands rolled themselves up neatly, until Sandry could put them into her pockets. She could always sew the lace onto new underthings.

There was a pair of scissors in her mage's kit. Sandry used them to cut up the panels of her silk underclothes. She returned to work, placing the new squares over the marks on the ground, then sketching the signs for protection and avoidance that would keep them safe. It took a little longer than using the ready-made cloths had done, but it was basic magic. She worked it quickly.

Her third rough-and-ready square was down when she noticed a black rim to the next mark on the flagstones. She drew closer, puzzled: what was it? This stuff was of the real world, not the magical one. It was just a thin stripe, outlining what looked like the side of a shoe. After a moment's thought, Sandry covered the entire thing. She then made her silk arch and stiffen like a bowl over the mark. She didn't want anything to touch that outline until the harriers saw it.

The next unmagic smear was clean — no dark rim. The one after it was not. Again, Sandry protected it with raised silk, and went on to the next. It was clean; the one after showed a heavier outline. Now she was certain: this was blood. The killer who cloaked himself in the absence of all things — unmagic, Wulfric had called it — was hurt.

On down the street she went, past the second barricade. The blood rim began to fade at that point: the killer must have bandaged his wound, though bloody traces still remained around the dark magic. Ten yards from the barricade, at the intersection with Silver Street, the marks ended. Sandry put her hands on her hips and glared at the last visible smear of unmagic. She didn't think the traffic on this larger street would have rubbed out all trace of those marks, so what had happened?

"Looks to me like he, or she, got took up — horse or cart," a crisp Namornese voice said at her shoulder. Sandry looked up at Wulfric Snaptrap. "You did nice work here," he added, pointing back down Tapestry Lane. Behind him two other Provost's Guards who wore the white trim of mages nodded eagerly. One was a captain, the other a lieutenant. They both carried heavy bags over their shoulders.

Sandry turned, to see a line of her silk squares dotting the walkway back to the barricade. "Oh, that," she said.

"Yes, that," Wulfric told her mockingly. He raised bushy eyebrows. For a moment he reminded Sandry of Niko, the gray-haired mage who had brought her to Emelan and served as one of her teachers. "Are you worn out?" Wulfric wanted to know. "Or can you help more? I'd like to get all this collected, and go over the house."

Sandry hesitated. Did she really want to go in that place? Hadn't it been bad enough, seeing Jamar Rokat in pieces?

But there was the matter of the unmagic smears. Every fiber of her being protested leaving them where they were. She rubbed her temples. "I need to send a note to Uncle," she finally said. "And if there's any tea about, I'd appreciate a cup." The lieutenant took a flask from her belt, opened it, and offered it to Sandry; fragrant steam scented with roseships and lemon curled from it. "You're a lifesaver," Sandry told the mage-lieutenant, who grinned shyly.

"She's Ulrina," Wulfric said, tearing a sheet of paper from his notebook and giving it to Sandry. "He's Behazin. They're my team for this sort of work."

When she had drunk her fill of Ulrina's tea, Sandry told Wulfric, "If I have to do for each spot what I did for that unmagic on Gury and Lebua, I'll collapse from exhaustion before we get near the house."

"I've been thinking about that," he admitted. "Here's my idea: instead of you weaving magic to bind this stuff, let's use these cloths you've put down as well as our own. Then we could mix up a blend of sweet pea, patchouli, and ylang-ylang oils —"

"Equal parts of each," suggested Captain Behazin. "So they're in balance." Lieutenant Ulrina nodded.

"And we work that into these cloths," Wulfric continued. "They're all attractors."

Sandry nodded. "That might do it. This unmagic is sticky to begin with. It wants to hold onto things."

Wulfric sent Ulrina for the supplies they would need. Behazin offered Sandry a bottle of ink and a brush for her note to Duke Vedris. As she wrote it, Wulfric ordered two watching Provost's Guards to move the barricade out to the intersection at Silver Street. All of Sandry's cloth squares were safe from the onlookers who gathered there now that the fire was under control.

When Sandry finished her note, she looked up. Wulfric was crouched by one of the bowl-shaped cloth guards — he seemed immune to Sandry's avoidance-spells. He was smiling. "What's so funny?" Sandry asked as she blew on the paper to dry her ink.

"I'm not laughing, my lady. I'm pleased at the turn in our luck. Our killer slipped up here, bleeding on the stones."

Sandry looked at him with interest. She'd been taught that things like hair, blood, and even clothing still had a magical connection to the person they came from. The kind of tracking that Wulfric could do was considered to be advanced, specialized magic — she had yet to learn how it was done. "Is there enough blood to use?" she wanted to know.

His grin broadened. "There wouldn't have been if everyone and his auntie trailed through before I got to it. Your quick thinking may have weighted the balance in *our* favor. We've enough here, and it's almost untainted. I should be able to track him quite nicely with this."

The image of Pasco dancing to call up fish rose in her mind. "Isn't there something else you could do?" inquired Sandry, her note forgotten. "Call him to you, if you have some piece of him?"

Wulfric shook his head. "It don't work that way. People don't want to regain whatever part of themselves they've lost — unless it's a limb. I could do it if he'd left a hand or foot behind. Otherwise it's the *part* that wants to go back where it came from, blood or hair or so on.

Spelled right, and put in a kind of compass, I'll hunt this lot to their lair." His grin broadened unpleasantly. "Then they'll answer for what they've done."

With the arrival of their supplies, the four mages — Sandry, Wulfric, and his two assistants — got to work. Wulfric and Behazin mixed the oils and called on their powers for attraction. While they did, Lieutenant Ulrina cut fresh squares so precise that Sandry knew she had spent hours learning to do just that, as Sandry herself had learned to make squares and circles. Once the mixed oil was ready, Sandry applied it to every fiber of her squares, and Ulrina treated the new ones.

When everything was ready, the assistants took a pile of cloths and headed for the site of the stable fire. Like Wulfric, they had spelled lenses that would help them to see the dark smears, now that they knew what to look for. Their job was to see if the fire had been set by an accomplice — "Elsewise," Behazin informed Sandry, "it's just too convenient" — and to gather up all the unmagic that he'd left there.

"Too much to hope the accomplice got hurt and is bleeding, too," Wulfric remarked, watching his assistants hurry off. "Still, no sense in overlooking the chance."

He and Sandry began to gather up the spots that Sandry had already covered. They worked their way back from Silver Street, entering the Rokat house and tracing the killer's movements inside. They did not enter the nursery. Instead they followed the set of tracks that led into that room on up to the roof, and to the building next door. They backtracked the killer further still, across a succession of rooftops. The trail led to another stable, down through a loft, and out onto the street, where it ended in a pool of unmagic.

"End of the road," Wulfric said gloomily. "Here's where our killer at least got all bespelled. I'm betting an accomplice set the stable fire, but he wasn't magicked here. If he'd been, his prints would be here, too."

"We'd better get all of this," Sandry remarked. She sent a goggling boy to a nearby draper's for a silk sheet, and paid him and the draper well.

That seemed to amuse Wulfric. "Provost's work's easier with you around, my lady," he told her as they waited for the sheet to soak up all of the unmagic. "If it'd been just us harriers, we'd've had to send back to the coop, and explain the expense to bookkeepers. With you, it's, we need it? Here it is. Let's get on with the job."

"I'm glad *you're* pleased," she retorted. She was tired. Only when she felt herself reaching for her friends did she realize they had fallen into the habit of borrowing strength from each other. No matter how hardworked any of them might be, at least one of the others would be rested and strong. Now she couldn't do that, and she missed it.

"I'm as grateful as I am amused, my lady," Wulfric said quietly. "Every time you make something like this a bit easier, that gives us more time and strength to deal with the real problems."

With the pool cleaned up, they returned to the Rokat house. Now they had to face that nursery. Though she wished that she could leave Wulfric to do this bit, Sandry knew she could not. The unmagic had to be cleared from the room so Wulfric could get information about the killer, and so that she would not have the creeping sense that it might blight anyone who touched it. Another team of harrier-mages, with lenses like those carried by Wulfric and his assistants, got orders to inspect every Guard who had entered the house. Those who showed marks were to be held until Wulfric could cleanse them. During the afternoon he'd told Sandry that Winding Circle's mages were working on something to get the stuff off human flesh harmlessly; clothes could be burned.

The blood-stink in the nursery was as bad as it had been in Jamar Rokat's office. Sandry told herself to be grateful that the bodies had been removed, but long splashes and puddles of blood told their own nightmare story. The pool of it in the crib was the hardest to bear.

By the time they were finished, long shadows told her

that night was coming on. Sandry was so weary she could hardly see as they left the house for what she devoutly hoped would be the last time.

Wulfric beckoned to Oama and Kwaben, who had spent the afternoon at the barrier, helping to keep out the curious. "Take her home," he told them as they brought the horses. "She's done good service for the realm today." He helped her up behind Kwaben: Oama would lead the horse Sandry was too exhausted to ride. "Don't you worry, Lady Sandry," Wulfric said. "Soon as I extract that blood from the unmagic, we'll be on these murdering animals like red on roses." He grinned fiercely and patted Kwaben's horse on the rump, sending them on their way.

Sandry napped during the ride to Duke's Citadel, but the clatter of metal on stone woke her. They were passing through the tunnel that was the short cut between the Arsenal and the palace. The noise did not end or even lessen once they rode through the outer curtain wall, which confused her. She looked around, bleary-eyed. Each of the baileys was ringed with torches, and there seemed to be an incredible traffic of wagons and people on horseback. She expected it to get quieter as they passed through the protective walls, but instead the noise grew. The innermost courtyard, before the main residence, was littered with animals, people, and baggage. She even heard babies crying.

"Kwaben?" she asked, peering around the Guardsman's back. "Where did all these people come from?"

He dismounted. When she slid from her seat, she staggered and would have fallen if Kwaben hadn't scooped her up in his arms. "I'm fine, you know," she told him sleepily.

She thought she saw a trace of a smile on his normally expressionless face. "You just can't stand up, my lady."

"What is this?" demanded Erdogun's familiar voice. "Is she ill? Make way, you people!"

Sandry roused. Here came her uncle with the baron. They were frowning. "It's all right, Uncle," Sandry assured the duke. "I've been working magic, and I'm a little tired. Didn't you get my note?"

"I got it," the duke said grimly. "Bring her inside," he ordered Kwaben. Turning, he bellowed, "Take these people in, *now!* Their goods may come later, but get them into quarters! Once they're in, put that barricade up!"

Two colonels, one in the uniform of the Duke's Guard, one in the uniform of the Provost's Guard, rode up to the duke and saluted. "We're ready, your grace," the Duke's Guard said.

"Then go to the city and relieve the day watches in the Mire and East District," the duke commanded. "My orders remain the same. I want those districts turned out for anyone who might be these killers. A house-to-house search, understood? Your people are under the authority of the coop commanders in each subdistrict. If you need additional help, send for it. Make sure watches are put on the sewers, in case they try to escape that way. Now go!"

"You see what kind of mischief he gets up to, when you're not here?" Erdogun muttered to Sandry.

She tried to sit up in Kwaben's hold. "Uncle," she said, raising her voice, "this does not look like resting to me."

He came back and laid a hand on her arm. "I will rest once these Rokats are safely housed in the inner keep," he told her. "It's the oldest part of the Citadel, one that's been spelled and respelled for protection for eight hundred years. Once I wake the magics, they will be safe until these murderers are caught."

"Whenever that may be," grumbled the baron.

"Uncle?" Sandry asked. She was afraid of what she would hear, but she had to know. "The — the man's head? Fariji Rokat's?"

The duke knew exactly what she meant. "Fountain Square," he replied quietly. "It was left on top of the memorial sundial."

The healer examined Alzena's wound carefully, her watery eyes nervous. "Very clean," she said, drawing vials from her bag. "No splinters, any dirt washed out by blood. No sense taking a chance, a' course."

She drew the cork from a thin glass vial and tapped a measure of powder first onto the wound in the left side of Alzena's calf, then the right. The powder foamed and hissed as Alzena's head jerked. She bit down hard on the leather strap in her mouth, smothering a scream.

"Well, that will do its work." The healer took a roll of linen from her kit and began to wrap Alzena's calf, keeping a watchful eye on Nurhar. She could not see the mage, hidden by his spells in the corner, but something was making her nervous. "All done," said the healer, tying the bandage off. "Give the medicine five days, then remove the bandage. I'll have my fee now — three gold majas, you promised."

Alzena clenched her hands in the bedclothes. The

woman knew they were illegal, and had demanded a price to match it.

Nurhar tapped Alzena's shoulder. "Is it well?" he asked. He could be asking about her leg, though he was not. She gave her head a tiny shake, and tugged the leather moneybag from her pocket. Her sword lay just under the blanket at her side like a promise.

Nurhar upended the bag in the healer's palm and fifteen gold astrels dropped out. "Count it," he advised. "You brought someone as guard?" The healer nodded. "There's a gold astrel in it for the guard if you can help us to Fortunate Wharf."

"Call him up. The man in green with the red cap," said the healer, too intent on the gold in her hand to use common sense.

Nurhar summoned him. The man hesitated at the doorstep, but entered when he saw Alzena facedown on the bed, the healer counting a heap of gold coins, and the gold coin that Nurhar offered him.

Nurhar was fast, nearly as fast as Alzena. The guard was dead in the moment between the closing of the door and his taking the coin. The healer started to turn when she heard him drop. Alzena flung the blanket aside as she rolled, brought out her sword, and beheaded the woman. She felt nothing but mild disgust: now they would have to wash the coins.

"Get rid of them," Nurhar told the mage, who came

out of the shelter of his spells. "Someplace where they won't be found."

"Salt," whispered the mage. His olive skin was ashen; he trembled. "I need a dose. My head's all woozy."

"*Get rid of them,*" ordered Nurhar. He went to sit by Alzena as the mage began to chant.

"Boots," whispered Alzena. The pain in her leg was fading. The healer's powder was doing its work. Her groping hand found one boot: she tugged it onto her good leg.

Nurhar reached for the other and dragged it to him. "What's this?" he asked, frowning. A dark stain ran down the leather into the crack where sole met upper. He glanced at Alzena, at her bootless foot. "Not blood?" he whispered. "You bled outside your boot?"

"So?" she demanded.

"*So?*" he cried, lurching to his feet. "Have you lost your mind? You left blood somewhere! They'll track us!"

Somehow it hadn't seemed important. It still didn't. "They have to find it first," she said, yanking the boot on.

The air in the room flexed, making her stomach lurch. They looked at the bodies, to find them gone. Only the blood of their victims remained, and the gold. "You have to get us out of here," Nurhar told the mage, sweat gleaming on his forehead. "She left tracks in her own blood for the harriers to find."

"*If* they find them," Alzena murmured.

"You promised salt," whispered the mage. He turned his gaze on Alzena. When had all the white vanished from his eyes? Now it was like staring into two vast pits. She turned dizzy, as if she might fall, when she met his gaze. Slowly she turned her head away.

"You'll have a full dose when we get somewhere else, mage," Nurhar barked. He frantically stuffed their belongings into packs.

"I don't know the town," the mage objected. "I don't know what's safe. I've only been to a few places, and I need salt."

Alzena reached into a pocket and produced a tiny silk bag. She waved it, letting the drug's pungent scent drift into his nose. "There's a safe place," she told him. "And you get this the moment you take us there, I swear on my family's honor."

The mage licked his lips. "Tell me," he whispered. Alzena did.

Nurhar gave the packs to her, and hoisted the carry-frame on one shoulder. He dumped the contents of two oil lamps on the bed and struck a spark with flint and steel. The oil caught, and started to burn. "Now," he said, coming to stand beside the mage.

In her dream she was back at the corner of Tapestry Lane and Silver Street. The pool of unmagic — But we gath-

ered it all, didn't we? her dreaming mind wondered —
had grown, spilling into the lane. She needed to soak it
up. . . .

She tripped. Down she fell, into that pool of nothingness. When she struggled to her feet, the dark stuff clung
to her.

The pool was far deeper than she remembered, up to
her waist. She fought, trying to wade out, but in this
dream the shadowy mess was thick and gooey, like syrup.
It embraced her, pulling her back into its depths.

She flailed and sank. It rose to chest level — no, to
her neck — no, her chin. Her fight to keep her head up
seemed to go on forever, until weariness made her body
ache. Suddenly Uncle was at the pool's edge. He waded
knee-deep into the unmagic, straining to reach her. She
opened her mouth to warn him, and the nothingness
flooded over her tongue; it poured down her throat.
Sandry gasped and choked. She couldn't breathe. Unmagic flooded her nose. She gagged, and felt it roll into
her lungs. . . .

Sandry woke. The nothingness loomed on every side
to swallow her bed.

She seized her crystal night lamp from the table,
holding it against her chest as she panted. The light
turned shadows into bed curtains. The dark at the foot
of her bed was the coverlet, turned back for this warm

Barley-month night. Her hands and nightgown showed pale, not dark. Sandry bowed her head over her lamp and waited for her nerves to calm.

When she felt more in control of herself, she got out of bed. Her small treasure chest was on a table by the window. She padded over to it, silently undoing the magic that locked it.

The item she sought lay at the bottom of the chest, under some ribbons, a few seashells, and what jewelry she kept with her. To most eyes the thing she lifted out of the box was only a circle of thread with four lumps spaced equally apart. To those who could see magic, the circle blazed with power, each lump showing a different color for each of four friends. To anyone who knew the laws of magic, it represented an achievement so great that it was already legend. Trapped underground with her friends during an earthquake, knowing they would die unless they could be made stronger together than they were singly, Sandry had taken their magics and spun them into one. This thread circle was the result of that, and the symbol of friends who were closer than family.

I wish you were *here,* she thought passionately, touching the lumps that represented Briar, Daja, and Tris. In those hard rounds of thread she could feel their powerful spirits. If we were together, we could stop these monsters. Instead it's just me, and I can't even *talk* to you. However am I going to deal with this unmagic?

She put the circle away and redid her locking spells. I don't *have* to manage the unmagic, she told herself firmly, settling into the window seat. The provost's mages will do that. All *I* have to do is teach a silly boy to keep a thought in his head longer than a sneeze.

Outside, the Astrel Island beacon shone over the harbor. The waning moon laid a silver blanket on the islands and the sea wall. She let the view calm her mind. She couldn't help Master Wulfric beyond what she had done already. Perhaps if she concentrated on Pasco, she would keep the boy from adding to the sum of all that was going on. Keep him out of trouble, she thought drowsily, cradling her night-lamp. Leave crime to the experts. And no more dreams about nothingness.

The next day Pasco was at Fletcher's Circle when Sandry and her guards arrived. Sandry eyed her student with dislike: she was still weary from gathering unmagic the day before. She had slept badly once she returned to her bed, and only the knowledge that Pasco had to be taught had gotten her on a horse that morning. He looked every bit as grumpy as she felt.

Sandry took him into the garden beside the eating-house — deserted at that hour — ordered him to sit, then placed her magical wards. Once they were protected, she sat beside him. "Let's begin. Close your eyes and inhale. One . . . two . . . three . . ." She stopped.

Pasco's shoulders were slumped, his face glum.

"You're not inhaling," she pointed out.

Pasco sighed, not looking at her.

Sandry gave a sigh of her own. "What is it now?"

Pasco shrugged sullenly.

"That's not an answer," she informed him.

"Uncle Isman came to supper last night," grumbled the boy. "He told Papa and Mama I must have talked you into saying my magic only works with dancing. He says nobody he's asked ever heard of dancing magic. He says, if I have magic, send me to the harrier-mages at Lightsbridge. He says they'll make me put my magic to the proper use."

"No, they won't," Sandry replied irritably. "You can only do that with certain kinds of magic. Others — the kind I have, the kind you have, only work through the path chosen by the magic. Your uncle may know all there is to harrier work, but he's no mage. He oughtn't to talk about things he doesn't understand."

Pasco scuffed his feet on the ground. "Why couldn't I be a truthsayer, or a tracker, or something? Then maybe they'd care. But no, what I have isn't good for anything *real*. I can't chill a riot or tell where thieves are hunting. So what's the point?"

"The point is, there is no point, not yet!" she cried, out of patience with the whole world today. "We don't *know* what you can do, you silly bleater! We're going to craft what you can do, and for that you'll have to help!"

Pasco stared at her. "You talked street," he whispered, shocked. "Bleater's no word for a lady to use."

"Mila of the Grain, give me patience," Sandry begged the goddess. It was time to try bribes again. "Pasco, if you don't work on meditation, I won't take you to your dance teacher today."

His gloom evaporated like mist in the sun. "A dancing teacher? With steps and music and costumes?"

"Meditation first," she told him firmly.

He sat straight on his bench, eyes blazing. "Meditation, definitely. I'm ready. I'm going to start now, watch."

They began again, and this time Pasco actually seemed to be trying. Sandry murmured instructions to clear his mind of all thought, and watched as his power trickled out of his skin, flowing away until it struck her magical barrier. It flickered and twisted or even went out completely, telling her he was thinking of something else. At moments like that, she began to see why some teachers were eager to use a switch on skittish students. She chided herself for the thought: that was just her weariness speaking, or at least she hoped it was.

Her own concentration was poor. Concerns about Wulfric's progress distracted her. She'd sent him a note asking if Rokat House and Qasam Rokat's home should be checked and cleansed of nothingness, with her offer of help. If he'd been right about the blood, Wulfric might actually have the killers by now. That would be a relief.

The clang of the Guildhall clock brought her to her surroundings with a start. The hour was done. Pasco's eyes were open and eager. "Lady — ?" he asked.

Sandry took up her warding circle. Returning her thread to her purse, she asked, "Walk or ride? It's not far."

Pasco looked at her guards and the horses waiting in front of the garden. "Walk. So who is it?" he begged as Sandry mounted Russet. "Is the teacher expensive? I can't pay, you know."

"We have an understanding," replied Sandry, clucking to Russet. "Come on."

"But *where?*" he pleaded, trotting alongside her. "Who?"

"He's chattery," commented Oama, looking down at the boy. "You sure he's harrier-bred? Usually *they* don't have two words to rub together."

Pasco grinned up at her. "That's 'cause they don't want the Duke's Guard blabbing their secrets."

"We'd have to be interested to steal them, boy," replied Oama with a wink at Sandry.

Festival Street was like most city roads, lined with

homes and businesses. The largest building on Festival between Market and Yanjing Streets sat behind a ten-foot-high stone wall. Sandry thought it may have been a warehouse at one time. Now there was nothing to indicate what use the building had. Its only marker was a painted sign over the gate — HEBET — in gold letters on a red background.

"Here we are," Sandry announced, guiding Russet into the courtyard. Oama and Kwaben followed. When she didn't see Pasco, Sandry turned. The boy was still in the street, goggling at the sign.

A girl came to take the horses when they dismounted. As she led the animals away, Sandry called, "Pasco."

"I'll get him," Oama said. She grabbed the boy's arm and towed him back to Sandry.

"Do you know whose place this is?" Pasco asked, his eyes fixed on the building.

"It's Yazmín Hebet's school, yes, I know," Sandry replied. Her earlier impatience was turning into amusement. *I might have acted the same if I'd heard of Lark before she took me as her student,* she thought. "I believe school *was* the idea. May we go in, please? There's an inside here. I'm sure you'd like to see it."

"She danced for seven kings in Aliput, and eight queens," Pasco babbled as they walked toward the open doors. "She danced for the emperor in Yanjing, just for him, for a whole year, and he made her a dress covered in blue pearls. Blue pearls, can you imagine! For dancing for one year for him and no one else!"

Inside, the door hallways pointed straight ahead and to either side. Open rooms on the halls emitted bursts of music from various instruments, many thuds, bumps, and squeaks, and shouts in male and female voices. At the end of the hall directly ahead, a dancer in leggings and a loose tunic tightly belted around the waist did a handstand, her legs pointed straight at the ceiling.

A boy in leggings and belted tunic raced by, stopped, and came back to them. "Was you lookin' for someone especial, my lady?" he asked, bowing low. His accent came from south of the Pebbled Sea; his skin was coal black like that of the tribesmen there.

"Lady Sandrilene fa Toren, and student, to see Yazmín Hebet," said Oama sternly.

The boy grinned. "Come." He raced up a narrow stair at the end of the right-hand hallway.

Following him, Sandry pretended not to hear Pasco's hissed, "I have a *name*, you know!"

She thought she was in fairly good physical condition, but she was panting when she reached the top of the stair. Their guide was not even breathing hard. He beckoned them down a long hall, past various rooms on either side.

"No, no, no, Thandi," cried a voice Sandry knew. "It's

turn turn *turn* jump, not turn turn jump. It's by threes, how many times do I have to — yes, that's right."

The boy led them to the room where Yazmín was shouting. He leaned in and said, "Noble in the buildin', Yazmín."

"Noble what in the building? Noble guard, noble lord . . ." Yazmín leaned out the door. "Wamuko, you have the manners of a goat," she told her messenger. "Lady Sandrilene, welcome." She came out and curtsied to Sandry, ran an appraising eye over Kwaben and Oama, then looked at Sandry's pupil. "Come on, Pasco," she said. "We'll start with stretches." She pulled him into the room.

"She knows my name!" Pasco whispered as he followed her.

The practice room was large and bare, paneled in golden wood and lit by large windows. The shutters were open, admitting a breeze. Benches were arranged around the walls. Sandry took a seat on one. Oama sat cross-legged on the floor beside her, while Kwaben leaned against the wall. Yazmín was giving instructions to three young people. When she finished, they nodded and trotted out. The flute player who had been in the corner went with them.

"Sit," Yazmín ordered Pasco. She pointed to the floor. Pasco obeyed. "Spread your legs as wide as you can. Wider. Here." She sat opposite him and stretched her own legs out until the balls of her feet pressed against the insides of Pasco's legs just above his knees. "Give me your hands," she ordered; Pasco did. She clasped him by the wrists and pulled him steadily forward, forcing his legs open wider. Finally he yelped. "Oh, you baby," chided Yazmín. "Look at you, not even a decent spread, and you're whimpering. Now hold that position."

"I think I'm stuck in it," Pasco squeaked as Yazmín eased back from him.

"Soon you'll be able to do this," she said, and swept her legs out farther still, until they formed a straight line with her body.

Pasco gulped.

Sandry heard a smothered noise from Oama, and looked down at her. The guard was chuckling.

"You'll also learn to do this." Keeping her legs apart, Yazmín lowered her body until she was facedown on the floor, her arms extended before her. "Now you try."

Pasco leaned forward gingerly, stretching out his arms. He rested his elbows on the floor.

Yazmín stood. She walked around behind Pasco. "Does that hurt?"

He shook his head.

"Well, it should," she informed him, and thrust down on his back with her palms. Pasco dipped several inches closer to the floor with a whimper. Without taking the pressure from his back, Yazmín leaned down and yelled,

"You want to dance? Work for it!" She took her hands away. "Sit up." He obeyed. She thrust him down again. "Dip. Sit up. Dip. Admire the sanding we did on this floor. It's splinter-free. Nice wood grain, don't you think? Sit up. Dip. I want you doing these exercises at home. If you don't, believe me, I'll know. That's enough for now — ten of these stretches at night. Get up."

Pasco winced as he pulled his legs together. "That *hurt*."

"Good," Yazmín said heartlessly. "Stand up. Touch your toes — don't bend your knees. *Touch* 'em, boy!"

She worked him for an hour, forcing him to bend his body in a number of painful ways. When a girl in pink ran in demanding that Yazmín come to settle an argument, Yazmín gave Pasco a corked flask and a drying cloth. "Breathe," she ordered, and left with the girl.

Pasco staggered over to Sandry. "She's a monster," he gasped. He worked the cork out of the flask and drank greedily. "A pretty, tiny, squeaky-voiced monster with muscles like a smith's."

Yazmín soon returned, a fiddler in tow. "Now, let's see you dance," she told Pasco. He glared at her, then lurched to the center of the floor.

Sandry got up. "Wait," she said. "Any dancing, he's got to be warded. We don't want what he does getting loose." She sent Kwaben and Oama to watch the door as the fiddler sat in the corner. Sandry created a circle big enough that Pasco and Yazmín could stay inside without having to worry about breaking the protection on the room.

For the next hour they reviewed common dances, ones Sandry had watched all her life without knowing that they had names or meanings. One dance was called "Dodging the Provost," another, "Bird in the Hand," a third, "Gathering Flowers." In that one the dancer skipped in a ring, plucking imaginary flowers from the air. Sandry thought Pasco might use that gesture to pull his runaway power back into himself. She wrote the idea down in the small book she now carried for just such thoughts.

While the boy danced, Yazmín had her eye on him, as well as her hands. She hovered, straightening his back, forcing an arm into a more graceful curve, putting more thrust into his spins. "Get your feet up!" she yelled. "It's a skip, not a shuffle. Show me air under your toes!"

When the Guildhall clock struck the noon hour, Yazmín called a halt. Pasco's hair and shirt were soaked in sweat. "I've never worked so hard in my life."

"That's what being a dancer is." Yazmín's dark eyes were kind and firm. "For you it's twice a problem. It isn't just what you do to survive, it's your power. And look at you. You're a fresh youngster, not an old lady like me, but —" She twirled seven times on the ball of one foot, lowered herself into a split, then raised herself again without once bending her knees. She leaned back until she could put her weight on her palms, raised her body into a handstand, then a split, then let her weight fall until she stood again. "I can do all that," she continued, breathing a little hard, "after chasing my lot all morning and getting *you* to stretch a bit."

Sandry took up her warding, trying not to smile. It really was too bad Yazmín wasn't a mage. If she had been, Sandry would have turned Pasco over to her without a qualm.

She was just putting her thread away when the lad Wamuko appeared in the door: he seemed to be the school herald. "His grace Duke Vedris," he announced, and the duke walked in. Yazmín curtsied as deeply as she had for Sandry, giving the illusion of wide, sweeping skirts when she had none. The fiddler, Pasco, and the guards all bowed.

Sandry grinned as the duke kissed her cheek. "I'd hoped you might still be here," he commented, "and since I was in the city on business, I thought we might take midday together." He bowed to Yazmín. "You are welcome to join us, Mistress Yazmín. The food at the Bountiful Inn is very good, and I would be honored to act as escort to you both."

Yazmín smiled at him. "If I may have a few minutes to change out of these things, your grace?"

He bowed again. "Please, take all the time you need."

Yazmín looked at Pasco, then at Sandry. "This meditation study you do before you come to me — if you like, I can save a room for you. That way you don't have to meet someplace, have one lesson, and then come here."

Sandry looked at Pasco. "What do you think?"

"Whatever you say, lady," Pasco replied, subdued.

"Then get here at nine tomorrow. We'll meditate before your dance lesson," Sandry ordered. As Yazmín and the fiddler left, Sandry added, "Remember to do those exercises tonight, before you get too stiff."

"I'm not stiff at all, lady," Pasco replied. "I'm weak as an overcooked noodle. Pray excuse me while I crawl home."

"A hot bath will help," Sandry pointed out as Pasco bowed first to the duke, then to her.

"Oh, good — a way to drown myself before I have another morning like this one." Pasco lurched out of the classroom.

"A message came for you from Master Wulfric just before I left the Citadel," the duke told Sandry. He gave her a piece of folded paper.

Sandry read it quickly:

Lady Sandrilene, greetings. I have read your note with regard to the unmagic that will be at Jamar Rokat's death scene and that of his brother. I have sent Behazin and Ulrina to cleanse the

164

street where Qasam Rokat was slain, since it is a public place. Keep in mind I cannot easily spare them, because drawing blood from the unmagic I presently have and preparing it for tracker spells is complicated work. Since Rokat House itself is locked and under guard with no one allowed in, I trust you will understand if we take care of tracking first, then cleanse Rokat House.

Your servant, Wulfric Snaptrap.

"Is everything all right?" the duke asked.

Sandry folded the note up with a sigh. "I'm just being silly, Uncle. Master Wulfric has everything in hand."

The duke might have pressed her about it, but just then Yazmín returned. She had changed into a crimson silk gown in the Yanjing style, made high at the neck and fitted to her body perfectly from shoulders to hips. She'd also done her hair so that curls tumbled out from under a shimmering gauze veil. The duke bowed over her hand, complimenting the dancer on so beautiful a change in so short a time.

"Performers learn how to dress quickly, your grace," explained Yazmín with an impish smile.

Even an ill wind blows some good, as Tris always says, thought Sandry as they walked down the street toward the inn. Pasco may drive me crazy, but I never would have met Yazmín if not for him.

She would light a stick of incense to Yanna the healer goddess, who was also the goddess of love. If the duke was paying attention to a lovely and spirited dancer, he might not spend so much time on paperwork or on worrying about murderers who seemed to walk through walls.

That night the dream began with Sandry in darkness up to her chin. She fought to keep it out of her face, but now she could feel unmagic seep through her very pores. She jumped out of bed and stumbled to the window. Leaning out into the cool night air, she gasped for breath.

Only when she was thoroughly chilled did she turn to sit inside her room. There was no sense in rushing back into a nightmare. Instead she got her notebook, ink, and brush pen. Pasco's bitter words about magic that did nothing to arrest criminals had been rattling about her head all day. So had the thought that stitch witches ought to be able to help provost's mages. She needed spells that would make her *and* her student feel they were of some use in this tangle.

The next morning Wamuko greeted Sandry and Pasco at the door when they arrived and showed them a tiny, empty room in the third story where they could meditate without interruption. At least Sandry could have done so. Pasco's inability to concentrate during their first lessons was nothing compared to his lack of attention now. Even though no classes were held on this floor, the noises made downstairs seeped under the door and through the floorboards. Pasco couldn't sit still: when Sandry caught him beating time to a faint tin whistle tune, she cast her magic more strongly into her wards, until no sound came in.

Now Pasco grumbled about the tailor's seat they normally used to meditate. Here at least she understood the problem. His muscles, unused to the intense work of the day before, ached. She sighed and told Pasco to sit in whichever fashion was most comfortable. After trying several positions, he decided that being flat on his back worked the best. He lay down as she began to count their breathing. As she counted, she let her voice fade, until they could breathe in the correct rhythm silently.

A minute or two went by without a twitch or fidget from the boy. Just as Sandry began to relax, Pasco yelped "Cramp!" He sat up, rubbing a calf muscle.

She sighed, and drew a thread from her purse. She tied it, imagining leg muscle around it, then undid her knot. Pasco gasped. "It just stopped!" he exclaimed. "I didn't think that cramp would ever —" He looked at Sandry, and saw the thread in her fingers. "Lady?" he asked.

"Would you at least *try* to concentrate?" she begged him. "I was ten when I learned. *Ten.* You're *twelve.*"

"Sorry, Lady Sandry," he mumbled. "I'll try. Really, I will."

They struggled through another half hour. Sandry was not sure which of them was more grateful when the Guildhall clock chimed ten.

"Well?" demanded Yazmín from the doorway once Sandry had gathered up her warding. "How do you feel today, Pasco?"

"Terrible," he said, approaching her warily.

She beamed. "Just what I'd hoped! Come on, and we'll do some stretches."

"Oh, good," Pasco mumbled as he followed her outside. "I *like* stretches."

Other students awaited them when they reached a second-floor classroom, all Pasco's age or a little older. Yazmín led the group through the same exercises she had taught Pasco the day before.

"At least he gets to see her torturing others the same way," Oama told Sandry quietly before she took up a watch-post outside the classroom.

Sandry giggled. Once she was settled on a bench, however, she concentrated on her notes. Awake before dawn, she had been staring at the harbor waters when she remembered the fishing fleet, about to sail after the day's catch. That had reminded her of Pasco's dance with the net, and that thought in turn had sent all kinds of ideas tumbling through her head. It had been all she could do to write them down then; now she studied them. Could a dance to call fish to nets be changed to

168

call humans to harriers? She would love to ask the Winding Circle mages about that.

Yazmín's voice broke into her thoughts. "My lady? Don't you have to do that thing with the thread?"

Sandry warded the room to keep Pasco's magic contained. Then she returned to her study of her notes. Maybe she ought to take a closer look at that special net they had used for Pasco's dance while she was at it.

Once again, Duke Vedris arrived at the school just as the city's clocks struck twelve. He invited Sandry — and Yazmín — to take midday with him. Following them out of the school, Sandry thought, If he keeps doing this, I absolutely must find an excuse to leave them alone.

The next day as Sandry, the duke, and Yazmín were finishing their meal at the Bountiful Inn, the door to their private room opened.

"Your grace, I tried to stop him!" protested the girl who had waited on them, trying to halt the intruder.

It was Wulfric Snaptrap. "And I told you I don't care if he's with an assembly of gods, I need to talk to him!" Bowing apologetically to the duke, he said, "Actually, to the lady." He nodded to Sandry.

She instantly rose. "I'm just finished, Master Snaptrap," she said. "Uncle, Yazmín, you will excuse me?"

Not waiting for an answer, she grabbed Wulfric and propeled him from the room in front of her. "I hope you didn't have anything drastic to say to Uncle as well, or if you do, you can say it in a note," she told Wulfric quietly. "I was looking for a polite way to leave. Of course, I really am at your service."

He looked down at her, eyebrows raised. "All I have to report to his grace is failure, and he never likes to hear about that. Do you think he's interested in Mistress Yazmín?"

"I devoutly hope so," replied Sandry. She steered him into the common room and sat at a table, pulling him down beside her. "Otherwise they'll think I've run mad. How goes the tracking?"

Wulfric propped his elbows on his knees and sighed. "It doesn't," he told Sandry, glum. "That blood's so tainted with unmagic that it's barely human anymore. We labored two straight days without a thing to show for it."

"Cat dirt," whispered Sandry, thumping her knees with her fists. "Cat dirt, cat dirt!"

"I use stronger words," Wulfric told her. "If only I could do something with all that unmagic we collected! There's what we took from Qasam Rokat's, and what my assistants brought from Fariji Rokat's, all nicely bottled, and there's not a thing I can do with it. Winding Circle still hasn't told me how to dispose of it safely, either." He ran his fingers through his gray curls. "My assistants are getting some rest. I thought if you were still willing, we might at least clean up Rokat House. So I'll feel I did something this week besides twiddle my thumbs."

"I know what you mean," Sandry assured him. "I would love to help." The night before, she'd had another dream of drowning in shadows. Maybe cleansing Rokat House would make her stop feeling powerless. "Have you enough supplies?"

"I brought plenty," Wulfric assured her. "Even if we run into a pond of the stuff." Sandry shuddered as he led her out of the inn and into the courtyard. Kwaben and Oama were there already with Sandry's mare; one of the hostlers held Wulfric's bony cob. "There's more news I didn't want to give his grace," he admitted as they mounted their horses. "The house-to-house search turned up three suspicious characters in East District. Looks like they had a healer up to see to one of them. They murdered the healer and the healer's guard, then set a fire to cover their escape. I'll let Captain Qais tell the duke about *that* mess." He flipped a coin to the hostler.

"If you could have used the blood to track them it wouldn't matter that they fled the inn?" Sandry guessed.

"Exactly," Wulfric replied as they rode through the gate. "But without even the blood to help, and with them getting away clean like that . . . His grace is fair, but I think I'll steer clear of him until I have some real progress to report."

What they had forgotten was that it was Lovers' Day. Long, long before, a noble maiden and a cobbler had drowned themselves rather than let their families marry them to others. For some reason their festival was marked by music, dancing, and a parade. Sandry's group had to muscle through the crowds. The din was worst in front of Rokat House itself, where the parade was passing.

The Provost's Guards on watch stood aside for Wulfric. He voiced the words that would break the magical seal on the door, though the sound was lost in the bang of cymbals and drums. When the wax seal crumbled away — the sign the magical seal had broken — Wulfric, Sandry, and Sandry's bodyguards walked inside and closed the door behind them.

It was pitch dark in the entryway — no lamps had been lit. Sandry pulled her lightstone out so they could see. Its glow revealed smutches of darkness on the stairs, on the wall, and on the railing. Holding the stone up, she could see more smutches along the hall that led to the rear of the building on the ground floor. She guessed the killers had escaped that way on the morning they killed Jamar Rokat.

Even with a wall between them and the parade, it was still hard for her to hear what the provost's mage was saying. Finally Wulfric put his mouth beside her ear. "Let's start with the worst of it this time, shall we?" He pointed upstairs.

Sandry nodded. She warned Oama and Kwaben to stay in the middle of the stair, and to sit on or touch noting until she had told them they could. They nodded their understanding. Sandry and Wulfric each hoisted a pack of the supplies that Wulfric had brought for the job, and began to climb.

Unbelievably, the noise was louder yet upstairs. Someone had left the shutters open on a window that overlooked the street from the hall.

Wulfric draped a silk square over his hand and opened the outer office door. "Ready?" he asked as he thrust it open.

She nodded and followed him, preoccupied with noting each and every place she could see unmagic smears. We'll be at this till nightfall, she thought ruefully as she waited for Wulfric to undo the seal on the room where Jamar Rokat had died. Once that was done, he stepped inside and halted. Sandry almost walked into his back. She frowned, reached to tap his shoulder — and Wulfric fell forward. Kwaben grabbed Sandry and yanked her away, into the outer office. She went down with a surprised cry.

Kwaben and Oama, swords drawn, jumped over Wulfric's body into the next room. Sandry heard the clang of metal on metal and lunged to her feet, running to the open door. A man and a woman, both strangers armed with curving swords, battled Sandry's guards.

"Mage, do something!" the woman shouted as she hacked at Kwaben. She was very quick. "Get us out of here!"

Once their basic studies were complete, all mages learned a few spells they could trigger in a hurry at need. Sandry used two of hers now. One raised a web of naked power between her guards and the strangers. The other sent a rope of magic snapping down the stairs. It blew open the front door, twined around the guards outside, and dragged them into the building.

Footsteps hammered up the stairs: her rope had worked, at least. Her web was not so effective. A hand with a sword in it darted through to slash at Oama; a hand with a dagger punched through next to the sword. The hands that clutched both weapons rippled with dark smears. Sandry could see a foot, a leg, a head as strangers attacked and retreated through her barrier. Riddled with the essence of nothingness as they were — as Wulfric had told Sandry their blood was — the strangers were able in part to reach through her power as if it did not exist. Kwaben and Oama could not cross her web at all, but they could and did battle the pieces of the enemy that got through.

Something, a rising force of unmagic, surged on the far side of Sandry's barrier. She thrust her web to one side. It yanked the strangers out of the way by pulling the real parts not yet consumed by unmagic. Oama and

Kwaben shifted with them, to keep fighting and to place their bodies between the enemy and Sandry.

Now the girl could see the rest of the room. Someone was against the far wall. He knelt — no, that wasn't right — he was *on* the floor, sitting, though she couldn't see his legs. The darkness pooled with him at its heart, unmagic streaming from his eyes and mouth to puddle around him.

"Come," he said. "Come away." He giggled. "Dihanurs, come now!"

Sandry tightened her web on the enemy, but they yanked free. They ran to the giggling man and sank in the dark pool before him. It was just like her dream, except they didn't fight the unmagic. With it marbling so much of their flesh already, they simply melted into the shadowy depths.

Their mage looked at Sandry. "They have the salt," he whispered, blackness rising around him. He toppled forward, into the pool. Some force — the hunger of unmagic for true magic — dragged Sandry across the floor, toward that empty gap. She screamed.

A hard arm wrapped around her waist and held on. The darkness sucked at her, trying to draw her into the pool. It was shrinking rapidly.

"Kwaben, help!" shrieked Oama as she clung to Sandry. They slid for an inch more; Kwaben stopped them. The unmagic vanished, leaving only a faint scum on the floorboards where it had been. Its grip on Sandry broke. She and Oama sagged onto the floor, panting.

"It was them, wasn't it?" Sandry heard Kwaben whisper. "The Rokat killers."

Sandry nodded. "Their mage called them Dihanurs, did you hear?" she said, when she could talk again. "They figured no one would search for them in a place where they'd already done murder, I bet." Then she remembered. "Wulfric!" Turning over, she broke out of Oama's hold and crawled over to the provost's mage. He lay in a pool of blood.

"Musta cut his th'oat as he coom in the doar," muttered one of the guards Sandry had dragged inside to help take the killers. They hadn't been able to get by Oama and Kwaben as they fought. "Bled 'im oat afore he knowed it."

"Gorry, they's fast," someone else whispered. "T'nail the ol' wolf like that. I seen him turn a spell on a copper bit, he were that quick."

Sandry rolled Wulfric over as tears streamed down her cheeks. She tugged her handkerchief from her pocket and tried to wipe the blood from his face. "Now you don't have to tell Uncle any bad news," she whispered.

A warm hand rested on her shoulder. It was Kwaben's; blood ran over it in a thin trickle. "Lady," he whispered sadly.

"I *liked* him." Sandry let her handkerchief settle over

Wulfric's open and staring eyes. She wiped her own eyes on her sleeve and struggled to her feet. "Let me see that arm," she told Kwaben.

She was no healer, but it was easy enough to lay silk threads from her belt-purse across the shallow gash over his bicep and use them like stitches to pull the wound shut. With that done, the bleeding slowed. Oama wrapped the arm in linen, and it stopped completely.

Sandry couldn't leave. There was the provost to be notified, and investigators to talk to. Waiting for them, she sat on a stool that bore no taint of the killers, and looked at the room. The Dihanurs had left their packs. That would give the Provost's Guards more information about them, maybe. Sandry doubted that any of it could be used for tracking, if their very blood was so corrupted by unmagic that traditional spells didn't work.

Of course these people would slaughter two children. The nothingness they used to slip by watchers and hunters was eating the Dihanurs, just as it had almost devoured the mage whose power came from it. It had taken enough of their life force away that Sandry's magical web could not capture and hold them. Next time her magic would probably be able to grip still less. Even if she could hold a small part of their bodies captive, how long would that last? And how on earth could that mage be captured?

The Dihanurs *had* to be stopped. Otherwise they would penetrate even the layered spells on the inner keep, where four families were hiding.

How to deal with that mage. How to deal with a mage and two killers who could reach through Sandry's magical barrier as if it were a net with large holes. . . .

There was a scrap of shadow inches from where she sat. It could be worked like magic, or the killers would not be able to wear it as a cloak. She could work her own magic like thread, and the magics belonging to others. Could she do that with unmagic?

Steeling herself, she reached into the dark smear and pinched at it with her fingers. As she pulled her hand away, it followed in a long strand like a fine grade of fiber. Goosebumps rippled over her skin — the almost-greasy, almost-sticky, whisper-sense of it on her fingers was very unpleasant — but she did not let go. Instead she twirled the strand as she might a tuft of wool, testing to see how easily it would spin. The strand turned as her twist traveled through it, thickening, just as wool might.

She got to her feet. "Everyone out of this room, right now," she said loudly. She turned, and held the eyes of the Provost's Guards with her own. She had to convince them that she was a senior mage and in total control, or they would never let her do this. "You can't see it, but the magic that lets those people get about unseen is smeared everywhere in here. It must be got up. That's what Master Snaptrap and I came here to do. If you don't want to track it all over Summersea, spreading gods only know what kind of ill power, then I've got to clean it up."

"But there's the investigators," objected the most senior of the guards present. He bore a corporal's yellow arrowhead on his sleeves. "They need statements from you and from your guards. That's how murder is looked into. There's the mages, who will try to see what happened."

"We *know* what happened," Oama informed the corporal. "We were right here." She looked anxiously at Sandry, who was digging in one of the packs Wulfric had brought. "You'd best do as she says, Corporal." She drew the man's ear down to her mouth, and whispered to him urgently.

From the pack, Sandry produced a bolt of spelled white silk. It had already been rubbed with the oil of attraction, so much so that it was already pulling the dark smears from her hands, arms, and the front of her gown onto itself. She marched out through the guards and into the hall with it. As she'd thought, the killers had kept to this part of the building — the marks they had left were confined to a small area. The hall that stretched toward the back of Rokat House and the stair that led to the third story were clean of unmagic.

Sandry threw the bolt of cloth into the long hallway, shoving it with her power. It unrolled to its full length, giving off a heavy, flowery scent. "Walk or sit on that, and nowhere else," she ordered the Guards. Returning to the packs, she found another such bolt, and spread it in the hall that led from the stair to the office. It moved as it settled over the smears of nothingness, pulling them from wood and carpet.

"I'll be in here," she told the Guards. They watched her with dismay. "Make sure the people who arrive know what I'm doing, and don't bother me."

Kwaben and Oama stood in front of the Rokat office, their faces mulish. "We are *not* going to leave you," Oama told Sandry. "What if they come back?"

"Then keep out of my way," Sandry advised them. "I have a lot of work to do in a hurry before you can so much as use these benches." Oama nodded and made shooing motions at the Guards.

Next, Sandry found canvas bags stuffed with spelled cloth squares in the packs. Placing one bag on the floor near Wulfric's body, she forced apart the stitches that held it together. A second unvoiced command, and squares flew through the room in a blizzard of white silk. They raced to cover every spot where Sandry could see unmagic. Taking the second canvas bag into the outer office, she did the same thing there. One canvas bag remained; she ordered its contents into the hall, where they draped themselves over benches and windowsill, sopping up darkness.

Walking back past Kwaben and Oama, Sandry noticed shadow smears on them. Getting a few extra squares of silk, she rubbed them briskly over her guards, collecting all of the nothingness she could find. Once she had it, she called one of the linen bags in the packs to her. It came, unfolding itself as it did. It blazed with signs for protection and enclosure written onto the fabric in the same powerful oils that filled every fiber. Sandry let it hang in front of her as she dumped the cloths she'd used on her bodyguards into the bag. Oama shifted; when Sandry looked at her, she realized that both dark-skinned guards were pale. They were staring at her.

"What's the matter?" Sandry demanded. "Why are you looking at me that way?"

To her surprise it was silent Kwaben who spoke. He said, "Lady, we knew you were a mage, but . . . Mostly you're like a cat with it. You never let it show any more than you can help, I think because you know it makes folk nervous."

"You only throw it around when you're upset," Oama added.

"I *am* upset," whispered Sandry. She plucked the linen bag from the air and went back to the inner office to collect the silk in there. She had to keep after the squares, to make sure they gathered *everything*.

Wulfric had brought plenty of those cloths, and plenty of bags to hold all they collected. Sandry blessed him as she cleaned, and tried not to look at him. That was hard, particularly when she had to slip a magical weaving underneath him, as she had first done at the castle infirmary, to gather the unmagic hidden by his blood and his body.

When all her silk was used up, she had to stop for a few minutes and think. She knew there was more nothingness in the building from the killers' earlier visit. She couldn't bear the thought of it lying about. Holding on to her last bag, the one in which she'd placed the two bolts of silk, she began to tremble. How would she get it all?

"Lady Sandry?" Oama whispered. She drew close to the girl, but didn't touch her. Summersea residents knew very well that it was a bad idea to bother a mage in the middle of a working. "Colonel Snaptrap's assistants came. They're gathering all the — the unmagic, they called it — on the stairwell, and on the ground floor. They said you should know."

Relief. Sandry rolled the top of her linen bag to close it. An order to the fibers in the cloth sent them weaving through one another. At last the bag was sealed as well as if she had sewn it shut with fine, tight stitches. Once that was done, she put the bag next to its mates, and found a chair for herself.

What next? she wondered, resting her head on her hands.

"Lady Sandry?" It was Oama again. She offered her water flask. "Captain Qais and his investigators are here. They got statements from the others and from Kwaben and me. You're all that's left."

She'd forgotten the Provost's Guards. "Tell them to make it quick," Sandry whispered. She accepted the water flask and drank deeply. If she hadn't thought it would be disagreeable, she might have poured water down her nose in the hope of rinsing away the stink of blood and death.

It wasn't the captain who questioned her, but the tiny woman with the seamed face and the old eyes. A scribe took notes as the investigator got Sandry to tell her story, from Wulfric's arrival at the Bountiful Inn to that very moment. Once done, she took Sandry over it again, making changes as Sandry added things she had forgotten or barely spoken of.

When she was done, the woman laid a hand on her arm. "You've been a very brave girl, my lady," she told Sandry warmly. "Captain Behazin and Lieutenant Ulrina said you were true to the heart and would never falter, and they were right."

Sandry blinked. "Oh. Thank you."

"My lady." Captain Qais had come in; he bowed to her. "All done?" he asked the investigator who had questioned Sandry. She nodded. He jerked his head toward the door. The woman bowed to Sandry and left, taking the scribe with her.

"Well," the captain said, his dark face wooden. "I must say, my lady, it would have been better if you had left this — unmagic — to Master Wulfric's assistants." The captain tucked his thumbs in his belt. "I am sure his grace will be most displeased when he learns of your involvement here."

Sandry rubbed her hands over her face. "At least you had the sense not to interrupt me while I was working," she informed the man, ignoring his indignant gasp. "And my uncle will understand why I involved myself. Pasco really is related to you? Because he's not at all stiff." She was being rude, as rude as her friend Tris. She would probably spend days writing a properly apologetic note after this was all over, but just now she didn't care.

"You are under a strain, lady." Qais appeared more wooden than ever. "I have told you, violent scenes like this are no place for a gently reared young woman. And while our family is gratified by your interest in my scapegrace nephew, it does no good to encourage him in his odd imaginings. Dancing, even dancing magic, whatever that means, will not clothe him or feed his children when he is a man. It would be better for you to send him to

Lightsbridge or Winding Circle for lessons, and for him to settle once and for all into the training he needs for real work."

Sandry got to her feet. This time she trembled with fury as she stared up into the captain's eyes. "Until you know more of magic, you will not voice opinions about it." Each word dropped from her lips like a chunk of ice. "For your information, I am proud and honored to be Pasco's teacher. He will be a credit to me. If he's a 'scapegrace' with 'odd imaginings,' perhaps it's because no one gave him reason to think he had anything good to offer." The captain came to a jarring halt against a windowsill. She had backed him out of the inner office and across the outer one. "He will *settle* for wherever his power takes him. And if the mages of Winding Circle temple can't tell where that is, I really don't think you should even hazard a guess. Am I done here?"

The captain nodded, tight-lipped.

"Then I have business that will not wait." Sandry looked around to see if she had forgotten anything. "Good day to you, Captain Qais." She strode out of the room and down the hall, ignoring the Provost's Guards who were there.

Wulfric's assistants were on the ground floor. She stopped to tell them where she had left the unmagic she collected. Even in the dim lamplight on that floor

Sandry could see that Ulrina's eyes were red and swollen from weeping. Captain Behazin's voice was hoarse. At Sandry's request they agreed to hold on to the stores of recovered unmagic that Wulfric had kept, as well as what they had gathered that day, until they heard from her.

"I'm so sorry," she whispered to them. "I wasn't quick enough — we had no idea they were here —" She squeezed her hands so tightly that her nails bit into her palms.

Both the captain and the lieutenant shook their heads. "It's this curst magic they've got," Behazin told her roughly. "We've no way to register it like we have other magics. He said he thought if anyone could think of a way to handle the unmagic, it would be you."

That was too much for Sandry. She bolted for the door, not even thanking Kwaben as he held it open. A Provost's Guard was holding their horses; when Sandry mounted Russet, the Guard gently patted her hand. She managed a smile for the woman, then turned her horse east.

"Shouldn't we go to Duke's Citadel?" demanded Oama, trotting her mount to catch up. "His grace will be fit to be tied if he hears of this —"

"I know, and I can't help that," replied Sandry, wiping her eyes on her sleeve. "I need to talk to the mage council at Winding Circle." She glanced over at Kwaben.

"You must see a healer about that cut," she said flatly. "Why don't you take word back to the Citadel that I'm all right?"

He shook his head. "There are healers at Winding Circle, aren't there?" he asked. "We can send a messenger bird to his grace."

"You *have* to keep us with you, Lady Sandry," Oama said. "Otherwise we could end up hanging over the inner gate by our ankles for letting you walk into a trap."

"I didn't —" protested Sandry. "You couldn't have — oh, never mind." She kicked Russet into a trot. The sooner she got to Winding Circle, the sooner she would know if they'd found a way to handle a mage who dealt in unmagic, or if she would have to try something of her own.

Please, gods, she thought fiercely, let them have a way to settle this. Please don't make me do it.

11

There was no way Sandry could break the news gently to Duke Vedris. "I'm going to lay a trap for the Dihanurs. The mages at Winding Circle think I have a chance."

For a moment there was only silence as the duke's eyes met hers. Then he said, "No. We have provost's mages, even battle-mages, with more experience in the taking of killers than you."

"This is different, Uncle."

"I forbid you to put yourself in such danger," the duke said tightly.

Sandry gulped and stood her ground. "I don't like it either, but I don't see another way. They must be stopped."

The duke turned his gaze to Lark, who stood just behind Sandry. "How can this be? Of all the mages at Winding Circle, how is my great-niece the *only* one who can handle this monster?"

"Not just me, Uncle," Sandry told him. "Pasco's going to help." The moment she spoke the words, she wished she could unsay them — or at least unsay her student's name.

The duke rested his shaved head on his hands. "That feckless, rattle-pated . . . Well. Knowing that he will assist you makes all the difference. Now, instead of *wishing* to throw Winding Circle's mage council into the harbor, I will do so. Immediately."

"Your grace, you know we can't allow that," Lark said gravely.

He looked up, and raised a finger. "Ah. You are powerful enough to stop me from tossing your council bodily into my harbor, but you tell me you cannot stop the Dihanur assassins and their mage. Can you see that I might feel somewhat — confused?"

Lark settled herself in a chair in front of Duke Vedris's desk. "You may as well get comfortable, dear," she advised Sandry. "He's going to be difficult." Sandry obeyed, taking the seat beside hers. To the duke Lark said, "We will do all we can — prepare the materials she needs, guard her and Pasco when the time comes, and dispose of what remains of the enemy's work. We won't send a fourteen-year-old girl and a twelve-year-old boy naked to do battle with a blighted mage."

"Strange," remarked Erdogun. He sat just behind the duke's chair. "That's what it sounds like to *me*."

Lark folded her hands. "You know I am classed as a great mage." The duke nodded. "I work spells by passing them through my thread. I *must* bind my power to real thread and whatever I use to handle it, or none of my spells work. That's true of every weaver-mage I know — except Sandry. She handles magic itself like I work thread. She can spin magic. She can weave it. She can embroider, or knot, or even tie a fringe with it, if she wants to —"

"Lark," Sandry protested.

"No, my dear, it's important that people know how unique your gift is. In this case it's vital — I'd hate to have to fight the Dihanur mage *and* his grace."

The duke smiled, but his eyes were grim. "I'm honored that you would think the task difficult."

"But why?" Erdogun demanded. "You're a great mage — your fellows on the council are great mages, legendary for power and craft. You have an arsenal of capture-magics and spells to drain the power of other mages. Do you really expect us to believe you people can't take this — fellow — and turn him into a tea cozy, if that's your fancy? However powerful this madman may be, I do not believe that he can stand against all of you."

"But he can," Lark insisted. "The nature of his magic is the absence of ours, don't you see? We could grip him with all we have, and he would not only walk away, but his magic would consume ours. Sandry got a taste of that

191

when the Dihanurs escaped. His unmagic almost pulled her into the door he'd opened."

"Then how will anything that my lady does trap him?" demanded Erdogun.

Sandry told the baron, "I'm going to spin his unmagic into a rope and knot it into a net. Then Pasco will dance the spell to bring the mage and the two killers to us. They won't be able to fight it, any of them, because they're all so tainted with the nothingness that it's like their own lifeblood. The unmagic net will pull them in."

"Once we have them, we can cleanse them," said Lark. "You'll have the killers for trial, and we'll keep the mage in custody. And it must be soon, before they can work their way through the layers of spells on the inner keep."

"What?" cried Erdogun, offended. "The inner keep is *impregnable* once the protective spells are activated!"

"It isn't impregnable to *this* mage, haven't you been listening?" Lark demanded. "Thank your lucky stars that he doesn't know the rooms where the families are kept, or he would simply walk through from where he's hiding now into those rooms. Once he tires of trying that, he'll just bring the Dihanurs here and send them through the spells. It may take them time to go through each and every layer — think of acid eating its way through a bolt of cloth — but eventually they'll get through."

"Are there are no spells against nothingness in the layers?" asked the duke quietly.

Lark shook her head. "To spell against it, you would have to use it — and then it would spread and eat all of the other spells." To Erdogun she said, "Must they break into this castle before you're convinced?"

"They can't," Erdogun said flatly. "You Winding Circle people are alarmists."

Someone hammered on the study floor. "Your grace! Your grace, please open up!"

Alzena was getting very tired of Duke Vedris. Putting all of the Rokats in one place for safekeeping should have been perfect for her and Nurhar, but this duke was an old fox who knew the ways of hunters. He had brought them into his own residence. Now they hid in the castle's very heart — a stone tower hundreds of years old, with more layers of spells to ward it than there were stars.

Why do this? Alzena wondered as she slid by the guards at the last gate to the duke's residence. Everyone knew Vedris only tolerated the Rokats for their myrrh. If he hated them, why bring them here?

She would kill him, when she was done with the Emelan Rokats — or she would if she wished. She cared about so little except that one goal, the end of these Rokats. The family had invested so much to send them here, the expense greater than that spent on the teams in any of the other Pebbled Sea countries. Jamar and Qasam had been the brothers of the Rokat who had killed Palaq Dihanur and displayed his head in dishonor; many of those now in the inner keep were the grandchildren of Jamar and Qasam Rokat. Their deaths came first; they had to. Only when the last Emelan Rokat was dead could Alzena tell this duke what she thought of his interference.

The numbers of people in this Citadel were a nuisance, but only that. She simply had to be careful that no one blundered into her.

At first the palace spells were laughable, cobwebs against her face as she climbed the steps to the duke's residence. The main doors were closed and guarded. Alzena waited. Sooner or later they would open — as they did now. A woman in servant's gray emerged, arguing with a pair of guards. Alzena slipped around them and went inside.

Today was a scouting mission only: with no palace maps available for study, one of them had to explore the place. Next time, when they were ready to finish their work, Nurhar would come to help with the killing. It was time that he did. Even she would not be quick enough to slaughter them all before someone thought to attack the place where she *might* be, or to throw a net over her.

Alzena found her way by feel, choosing her direction by the number of cobweb-magics that brushed her as she walked. The thicker they felt, the closer she was to her quarry. On she trudged, eyes straining as she peered through the slit in her spell-mask. The feel of cobwebs got heavier; it took more and more effort to walk through them. The very air gained weight, until she could manage just one labored step at a time.

That would happen, the mage had said. She would never meet anything so complicated as the inner keep's layers of spells unless she penetrated some other ancient kingdom's private stronghold. They could slow her, but as long as she pressed forward, they would not halt her.

The air pressed more thickly against her body. She fought to go on — why? Was there a point? Yes, she remembered dully, the killing to come. Once it was done, she could stop. She could do nothing. No one would insist that she get up, walk about, eat, dress. They would leave her alone. That would be good.

She knew, in the part of her that said she used to love Nurhar, that she owed everything to the family. House Dihanur had saved Alzena when her parents were murdered, had raised and taught her, had given her a husband. Dihanurs had gone to the expense and loss of family lives it took to capture the mage and ensure he would obey her. They had bought dragonsalt to keep him dependent on Alzena and Nurhar. Without it, who could say whether he would stay grateful to those who'd saved him from the pirate who crippled him?

Alzena halted, fighting to breathe under the weight of magic that encased her. The hall had opened onto a broad, wide corridor that followed a curved stone wall. She could see that wall only near the ceiling. Its stones were so black and pitted that they had to be the stones of the inner keep. The rest was hidden behind a wood barricade ten feet high. It reached as far as she could see in both directions; she would have bet that it went all the way around the inner keep.

How dare they add one more obstacle, even one as stupid as a wooden fence? It could only slow her down, but it could never stop her. Alzena's eyes were fixed on the thing, already examining it for weakness. If she could not wait until someone opened the lone door in the barricade and slip in that way, she might have to climb it. Calculating, she didn't see the low, treacherous step down to the floor that wrapped around the inner keep. When she missed it and stumbled, she made a perfectly audible thud.

The six guards loitering around the door through the barricade sprang to their feet, drawing their swords. They spread until they were within sword's reach of one another, sweeping in front of them with their weapons.

One of them blew a shrill blast on the whistle that hung around his neck.

Oh, they had been well briefed, and she had been a fool to let a sound escape. They knew they might not see her, but they could slice her, just as the arrow had punched through the spells and into her flesh. If she had been quiet, if she had not missed that step, she might have worked her way around them. She could have gotten to the door and slipped in, just as she had walked into this building. They were ready for her now. The guard at the end of their line stayed within sword's reach of the door.

She turned away in disgust, and blundered into three guards who had been hidden by yet more spells. The sight of their comrades coming to alert had brought them out of their concealment — or had they, too, heard that stupid noise of hers?

The layered magics dragged on her as she drew her sword and cut down the one she'd run into. She chopped at his neighbor's leg; the woman fell to the floor. The third guard who had been hidden swept his blade from side to side, feeling for her. Only a few inches lay between Alzena and his weapon, and she could hear running footsteps. Reinforcements were on the way.

She oozed back from the guard whose blade sought her flesh. The guards on the barricade were advancing carefully. Older and wiser than the one she had killed, they were leaving no room for her to get by them and through the barricade door. She backed down the hall, her sword ready, glancing back twice to make sure she walked into no one else. Fresh guards poured into the area around the barricade from an adjoining hall.

"There," one of them said, pointing. Alzena looked down and shook her head. Her sword was dripping, leaving a blood trail. She dropped it and continued to back out, moving faster as she put distance between her and those cursed spells.

She had to stop in the main hall, when a trickle of warmth down her leg told her she was bleeding. One of the guards had cut her side. Cursing under her breath, she filched a lace runner from a side table and wadded it against the cut, tightening her belt over it until the thing pinched. Only when she was sure that she wouldn't leave a trail did she make her way out of the residence.

She had plenty of think about as she inched by milling guards, placed on the alert by their comrades at the inner keep. She and Nurhar could manage the layered spells, but what of the barricade? The guard on that small door would be doubled, and it would be alert — these people were very well trained. She and Nurhar would have to climb the barricade, which meant they would need tools, and the mage to hide the noise they made. And if she had discovered anything about these people, it was that they learned from their mistakes. Next time it would be harder to get as close to the inner keep as she'd done today. She had to find another way in.

For a long, long minute after the messenger told the duke that one guard was dead and another wounded in the inner keep, no one made a sound. Sandry rested her hands on the duke's shoulders, not liking the expression in his eyes. She knew this had to cut deeply. An assassin had made his or her way to the very heart of Vedris's power. Erdogun's brown face was tinged scarlet with humiliation at being proven wrong almost as soon as he had called Lark an alarmist.

At last the duke looked up at Sandry and gave her a thin smile, patting one of her hands. "Must you do this with Pasco?" he inquired. "The boy is nice enough, but he doesn't seem very reliable."

Sandry glanced at Lark. "We did talk about another way, but —" She swallowed. "Truly, Uncle, I prefer this."

The duke frowned. "What is this other way that you find so distasteful?"

Lark sighed. "We discussed shaping the unmagic as a web, rather than a net, and blanketing the inner keep with it, like a spider's web. When the assassins come, they'll touch it and — well, they won't stick to it, exactly. The nothingness in them would become part of the web."

"Then I could take the web and unravel it, maybe

even spin it into one cord," Sandry explained. "The problem is, Uncle, I couldn't save the parts of them that are still real. If I had to do it that way, I'd kill them — if it even worked."

"We *know* the net-spell will do the job," Lark assured the duke. "And if Pasco calls these people to the net, we can make sure no innocents will be trapped. We'll meet the Dihanurs on our terms, not theirs."

"Have you spoken to Pasco?" asked the duke wearily.

"No," replied Sandry. "I wanted to work it all out before I talked to him."

"He'll refuse," Erdogun said tartly. "If he has a whit of sense, he'll refuse."

12

"I could help catch rats?" Pasco demanded, eyes alight. It was the next morning, at Yazmín's school. "By *dancing?*"

"That's the idea," Sandry told him.

Pasco jumped up gleefully. "That will show them!" he cried. "Tippy-feet indeed!"

Sandry looked at her hands and smiled. She had thought Pasco might see it that way. "We're not *sure* we can do it," she warned. "I still have to make the net."

"But you will, and I'll dance it, and we'll have rats in it. A nice day's fishing for a fa Toren and an Acalon, don't you think?"

Sandry grinned at him. "I *do* think."

Pasco carefully lowered himself into a split, wincing as he completed it. "We can do it," he told her, his face serious. "You can do anything."

"We'll see," she replied. "It may come to nothing if I

can't work that stuff into a proper net. Now settle down. Let's try meditation."

He did a little better today. Sandry could see his magic did not stray so far from him. It also didn't flicker as much as it had, which told her that his attention wandered less. *Maybe he just needs something useful to do,* she thought as the city's clocks chimed the hour. *Something his family thinks is useful, anyway.*

As she took up her ward and Pasco stretched his legs, Yazmín walked in. "You said when you got here that you've something important to discuss?" she asked Sandry.

"We're going to make a net-dance for rat-trapping," Pasco told her cheerfully. "And I'm going to dance it."

"It's a way to catch these killers," explained Sandry. "If you don't mind, we'd like your help with creating the dance, and getting Pasco ready for it. Everything has to be planned to the inch. One wrong step — if he so much as brushes the unmagic —" Sandry gulped. "I think the net would devour him."

"Never fear," Yazmín said cheerfully. "I can get him so he'll be able to hit a dot on the floor, blindfolded, every time. A small dot." Pasco sat with his left leg straight out in front of him as he tried to grip his foot and touch his forehead to his knee. Yazmín pressed down on his left knee with one hand as she pulled back on his toes, forcing him to stretch an extra inch. He whimpered, then touched his forehead to his knee and held the position to a count of ten.

Sandry watched them solemnly. "If you've any doubt he'll be able to do it, I have to know right now," she told Yazmín quietly.

The dancer looked at her and smiled. "You're using that dance he showed me the other day as the basic, right?"

Sandry nodded.

"How long till you're ready to go?"

"I want another look at the net he used for the fishing spell," Sandry replied. "I'll do that today, and I'm to help Behazin and Ulrina — the harrier-mages — distill the rest of the unmagic out of what Master Wulf —" a lump rose in her throat. She coughed to clear it, blinked rapidly until her eyes didn't sting any more, and went on — "out of what was gathered yesterday. Tonight I'll sketch a rough net for us to look at in the morning. We'll work on the dance while everything else is being made ready at Winding Circle — two more days, I think. And you can work with Pasco some more while I spin and make the net. Will that be enough time? Three or four days?"

"I'll spend every waking minute with our friend, here," Yazmín said with a wink to Sandry. "I'll give him all the personal attention he can stand."

Pasco, switching to stretch his right leg, muttered, "I'm doomed."

Do they really understand how serious this is? Sandry wondered as she set about creating a permanent warding on a room for Pasco and Yazmín to work in. Do they understand that if he touches this net he can't even see, the power of his dance combined with the net will eat him up? Should I talk to them about it some more?

She was still wondering as she told Yazmín how to activate the wards on the room without a mage present. Yazmín tried it a couple of times, raising and lowering the protections that would keep Pasco's magic from spilling out. Then she rested a hand on Sandry's arm.

"I know you're worried about precision," she said quietly in her odd, cracked voice. "But really, take my word for it — enough practice with an accurate drawing of the net, and he'll hit his marks every time. He's got body memory, better maybe than mine. I don't know if that's because he'll be a fine dancer or if the magic helps him. Either way, you won't be taking a foolish risk, using him."

A bit of Sandry's worry evaporated. "Thank you, Yazmín."

The dancer flapped a hand — no thanks necessary — then entered the warded room with Pasco. "Come on," she cried gleefully. "I've got you all to myself. We'll do some real work now!"

"That's what I'm afraid of," muttered Pasco.

*   *   *

Sandry's visit to the fishing village turned out better than she had hoped. Grandmother Netmender was quite willing to let her examine the net that Pasco had used to dance for fish. Able to inspect every inch of it, Sandry found that some of the net's power lay in the unusual knots that held the rope squares in place. The old lady taught her how to tie them, making her practice until Sandry could do each of the three different knots perfectly. Sandry could see that when she tied these with unmagic and combined them in her net, she would double her spell's power.

From the fishing village she rode to the Market Square coop, where Wulfric's office and workroom had been. There she talked to Behazin and Ulrina, who promised to distill the unmagic from the silk they had gathered at Rokat House the day before. She also looked at the stuff collected earlier, which was kept in spelled glass bottles. Since there was no weight to the nothingness, there was no way to tell how much they had, but Sandry was sure that with the unmagic from Rokat House, she would have enough for her net.

When they finished, they tidied up and went to the temple of Harrier the Clawed for Wulfric's last rites. Harrier's worshippers saw no point to burial or to preservation of a body for several days while mourners came to view it. They expected to join their god the day after their deaths. With the other mourners at the temple, Sandry made an offering of feathers and incense in Wulfric's name. A priest called for testimony of his service to the god. Then the lady provost Behazin, even two dedicates from Winding Circle — Moonstream, the dedicate who ruled the temple city, and Crane, head of the Air temple and a friend of Wulfric's — all spoke about his honors and the work he had done on behalf of Summersea.

The duke spoke last, and simply. "Murderers have taken the best harrier-mage I have ever known," he said, his voice ringing from the temple's stone walls. "They shall pay for it."

Sandry fought tears all through the ceremony. Tears would just make her weak, she thought, and she had to be strong for the work ahead. They came anyway, as the acolyte set Wulfric's funeral pyre ablaze. Sandry hadn't realized the duke and Baron Erdogun had come to stand with her until Vedris put his arm around her. She leaned against her great-uncle for a moment, then straightened, and blew her nose. Watching the flames rise around Wulfric's body, Sandry made him a promise: she would snap the trap on the killers and their mage.

That night she dreamed she drowned in unmagic, trying to scream when it flooded her mouth. She got out of bed and worked on her plans for the net until dawn.

She rode with the duke, took breakfast with him and Erdogun, then went straight to Yazmín's. There she sketched the dimensions of the net on the workroom floor, using a measuring cord and chalk to lay out the design. Once it was perfect, she took a roll of scarlet ribbon and laid it over the chalked lines, then smoothed it down with her magic. Pasco, ever curious, tried to peel the ribbon off the floor, without success. He couldn't even get a corner free of the wood.

"I'll take it up again, after," Sandry promised Yazmín.

"I don't know," the dancer said, raising the wards on the room so they could get to work. "It's a bit of pretty."

They meditated first — to Sandry's surprise, Yazmín had been trained in it. Then Yazmín and Pasco showed her what they had done on the net dance. The three worked on shaping it, crafting each step. They stopped to eat their midday and then returned. With the dance itself set, Yazmín went to work on Pasco. This was the time for him to learn precision. If he so much as brushed the edge of a ribbon square, Yazmín was on him like a tiny wildcat, scolding furiously and positioning his feet and body with rough hands.

That night Sandry dreamed again of the lake of darkness swallowing her. This time she sat up, walked around the room, splashed her face with water, then tried to go back to sleep. Twice more she dreamed of unmagic, waking in the dark as she gasped for air. She fell asleep again near dawn and slept for several hours, dreamless at last. Her attempts to scold the servants, Erdogun, and her uncle for letting her sleep late were ignored. When she got to Yazmín's, she discovered that the dancer and Pasco had already meditated in the protected room and were working on the dance-spell.

When they came back from midday, the boy Wamuko gave Sandry a note. It was from Captain Behazin: he and Ulrina had distilled and bottled all the nothingness they could find. Two hours later a courier from Winding Circle arrived with a package for Sandry. Wrapped in canvas, it had spells of protection and cleanliness laid so thickly on it that looking at it too often left spots on Sandry's vision. She sighed. Of course they would spell everything for this working with all the strength of the Winding Circle mages — she just hadn't realized what that would do to her poor eyes. She cleared her mind, then drew a kind of veil over her sight, one that would shade her eyes from the brightest magical fires.

When she opened them, the blaze on the package was dimmed to a pearly shimmer. Opening the canvas wrap, Sandry found a note:

The tent is being raised on the spot we discussed on Wehen Ridge. Unless I hear from you otherwise, I will meet you there at eleven of the clock tonight with your remaining supplies.

Gods bless

— Lark

"What is it?" Pasco reached for the sturdy, pointed, two-foot-long dowel rod that was part of the package's contents.

"Don't touch that!" She smacked his hand gently. Pasco jerked it away and stuck his fingers in his mouth. "Oh, stop it," Sandry told him, exasperated. "You aren't hurt."

He took his fingers from his mouth and asked, "So what's all this for?"

"The rod's the stem for a drop spindle. It fits through here —" She picked up the second piece of wood in the canvas, a flat round piece six inches in diameter with a hole in the center. She inserted the pointed end of the rod through the hole. Three inches down the rod's length, the round stuck. Assembled, the spindle looked like a very large top with an extra-long stem.

"My aunts and cousins and the maids use those, but theirs are smaller," Pasco remarked.

"Mine's bigger because I'm doing cord, not thread." Sandry ran the oversized spindle through her fingers. "And I'm in a hurry."

Winding Circle's carpenters had done a beautiful job.

First they had carved strips of ebony, elder, and willow, all magically protective woods, to fit together into a rod and a disk without using glue. They had done so precise a job that Sandry couldn't take the pieces apart. The rod and disk might as well have been made of solid wood. Moreover, the carpenters had laid more signs of protection, strength, and cleanliness on their work. When Sandry spun the unmagic, all of it would go into her cord and only her cord.

"It's beautiful," commented Yazmín, leaning over Pasco's shoulder to look at it. "They do nice work at the temple." Her brown eyes met Sandry's. "This is it, right? You have to start."

Sandry nodded. She wrapped her spindle in canvas and tied the package up again. "I should be ready for Pasco tomorrow." If nothing goes wrong, she thought nervously. If I don't mess things up.

"Well, then, Pasco, come on — enough loafing." Yazmín rapped the boy's head with her knuckles and moved out to the corner of the ribbon net. "I want to see that jump again, and you'd better hit the mark clean this time."

"You turned me over to a monster," Pasco grumbled to Sandry as he got up.

Sandry patted his bare feet. "But she's doing you so much good," she told her student in her cheeriest warm-and-supportive voice.

By now Pasco knew her well enough to know she was teasing. He sneered at her and walked up to the ribbon set. Sandry got to her own feet again, and left them to their practice.

The duke rode with her to the ridge that night. She had argued fiercely against it — rain had already begun to fall, drumming on roof tiles, cobbles and on the canvas hood of the cart that held the bottles of unmagic — but in the end she had to admit defeat. Duke Vedris had decided to keep watch with Lark as Sandry did her dangerous work, and there was nothing Sandry could say that would make him remain at home.

They rode in silence beside the cart, which was driven by Kwaben. Oama sat beside him. When Sandry saw them on the driver's bench, cloaked and hatted against the rain, she tried to protest that as well. The look they gave her, as if they dared her to comment on two of the most elite unit of the Duke's Guard serving as common wagoners, convinced her that she would be as successful at talking them out of it as she had been with her great-uncle.

If the truth were to be told, she took a great deal of comfort from their presence and the duke's during the long, wet ride through Summersea and the Mire. The squad of the Duke's Guard behind and on either side of them was also welcome.

It's not as if I've never been terrified out of my wits before, she thought as they began to climb up the road between Summersea and Winding Circle. Even before the year of disasters — earthquake, pirate attack, forest fires, and plague — that cemented her bond with her three friends, she had known trouble. Her parents had died in another plague almost exactly five years ago. As travelers her family had survived gales at sea, ice storms, pirates, and robbers. Sandry knew fear and disaster well.

But this is the first time I've ever grabbed danger with both hands and hugged it close, she thought, craning to see through the veils of rain ahead. "There," she said, pointing at a line of lamps off the road to their left.

"I see them," Kwaben replied evenly. His big hands were steady on the reins.

"It isn't raining *that* hard, my dear," added the duke.

Sandry looked at him and shook her head. Even in a broad-brimmed hat to shed the wet he looked dignified, even solid. It was hard to think he would let anything go wrong — except, of course, it wasn't up to him. It was up to her.

"You couldn't ask for a better night," Oama commented drily. She turned to look at Sandry. "Pity your mate Tris isn't here. She'd whisk all this damp off like a maid with a feather duster."

Sandry had to smile. She'd seen Tris do exactly that, with the same cross expression on her face that she wore when dusting. "She might disappoint you," Sandry told Oama. "These days she worries a lot about not interfering with the natural order of things."

"Exactly as I suspected," remarked the duke. "Too much education does ruin a perfectly good mind."

Sandry giggled as Kwaben clucked to the mules and turned them onto the path marked by the lanterns. She and the duke followed. When the cart drew to a halt, Sandry dismounted from Russet, taking the canvas package with her spindle out of her saddlebag. Robed and hatted dedicates came to take charge of the spindle and of the bottles in the cart while Sandry viewed the newest part of Winding Circle's contribution to her working.

It was a large tent with a smaller one attached to it as a lobby. They were anchored to a single flat slab of the rock that shaped Wehen Ridge, a barrier between Winding Circle and the slums of the Mire. The bonds that held the tents to the rock glowed silver in Sandry's vision, as did the tents themselves. They had been spelled so powerfully for protection that once more Sandry had to shape a magical veil to protect her sight.

"Sandry, welcome," said a cloaked and hooded figure. It was Lark. She looked startled when she realized who had come to stand next to the girl. "Your grace, you — you shouldn't —"

The duke looked at her mildly.

"Oh, what was I thinking — of course you would come," Lark said with a rueful smile. "But you'll have to part company here."

"I know it," replied Vedris. He wrapped Sandry in a tight, warm embrace. "If you get yourself killed, I shall be very disappointed in you," he said quietly, for her ears alone, and kissed her forehead.

Sandry attempted to smile, and gave it up when she felt her mouth wobble. "You know I try never to disappoint you, Uncle." She turned to Lark. "Shall we start?"

Lark led her to the smaller tent and kissed her cheek. "Don't worry about his grace," she told Sandry quietly. "Those of us who are standing guard have a snug shelter right behind this tent. We'll try to send him home, of course, but at least he'll be warm and dry until then."

"Thank you so much," Sandry replied as she stepped into the tent. "That *is* good to know."

"Hand out your clothes," Lark said as she closed the opening. "And gods bless."

This tent was divided in two: half was the kind of rough shower used by those who worked with the sick and wanted no taint of disease to cling to them. Sandry pulled the flap shut, then hurriedly stripped off her clothes and undid her braids. Her teeth were chattering by the time she finished.

"Lark?" she called.

Hands came through the opening in the flat. Sandry filled them with her clothes and shoes. Lark took them away.

Putting it off won't make me any warmer, Sandry thought, shivering, as she stared at the rope pull that would start the shower. I have to be cleansed.

Drawing the gods-circle on her chest, she gave the pull a hard tug. Slats on the wooden platform that roofed this tent opened. She was doused not with buckets of water, as she had expected, but with tubs of it. She sighed in gratitude: the water was just hot enough for comfort, and warmed her nicely. It had been mixed with yarrow, agrimony, willow, and elder for cleansing and magical protection. From the way it shone even through her closed eyes, Sandry guessed that Lark had taken the herbs from stores laid up by Briar and Rosethorn before they had left. It was like being home at Discipline again, and comforted her just as much as it warmed her.

The slats overhead closed and Sandry waited for the tubs to be filled again. Everyone had agreed that two rinses would serve to get all outside influences from her skin. Looking around, she saw that the tent was floored in more cloth. Like everything else around her, it was spelled to keep bad influences out, and any stray magic she did in.

No wonder the temple-mages had needed three days

to prepare — they were leaving no room for mistakes, and no chance that the unmagic would escape Sandry. That made her feel better, too. Working alone, she might have forgotten something. Instead, all she had to worry about was her spinning and the net. She prayed she could do it quickly: she wouldn't be able to eat, drink, or leave the larger tent until her finished work was safely packed in the box that had been made for it.

"Ready again," a voice called. Sandry yanked the rope pull, bringing the next flood of water down.

Once that was done, she opened the flap that divided the small tent in two. In the dry half, a long, sleeveless robe of undyed cotton was draped over a stand. She put that on and walked through into the large tent.

It was floored in cloth and secured to the rock platform, with no openings but the one she had just used. At the center was a chair and a stool on which a large, shallow iron dish was set. The bottles of unmagic were placed by the dish. Beside the chair was a wooden stand with sockets into which six long spools had been fitted. She also saw the box that would hold her net: it was ebony and spelled like everything else for protection.

Placed at regular intervals around the tent were round crystal globes that threw off both light and warmth. Seeing them was like feeling Rosethorn and Briar in the shower herbs. Those globes had been Tris's and Daja's work all last winter, as Tris supplied the light in the crystal and Daja the warmth. Someone had gone to a great deal of trouble to make this place homelike. On impulse Sandry reached with her magic to touch the cloth of the tent and its floor. It had been woven by Lark; the signs and oils that coated the fabric and kept out the damp were hers.

"Thank you, Lark," Sandry whispered.

Resting a hand on the flap that covered the opening to the smaller tent, she voiced the word "Secure." Winding Circle's mages had set the wards for her as she had done for Pasco and Yazmín, putting more strength into their guardian spells than Sandry could spare just then. Once she spoke the key word, *Secure,* the flap merged with the cloth walls and the wards blazed into life. She needed to draw yet another magical veil over her vision to keep from being half-blinded.

"Now comes the hard part," she murmured, but somehow the prospect wasn't as scary as it had been earlier that day. Rosethorn, Briar, Tris, and Daja were all around her; Lark was in the tent and holding vigil outside with the duke. Winding Circle's mages had done their best to shape this place for complex magics. In putting forth so much time, effort, and power, they had as much as told Sandry that they believed in her.

Don't make a muddle of this, she told herself now, picking up a bottle. There are fifteen children in the inner keep at Duke's Citadel. Whatever their parents and uncles and second cousins have done, they don't deserve to die for it, and you won't let them. You'll do this right, that's all there is to it.

She broke the wax seal on the bottle and pulled out the stopper, then upended it over the iron dish. Out flowed darkness like syrupy ink. One bottle filled the dish.

Earlier Sandry had prepared her spindle with a length of undyed, purified cotton thread. It was called the leader, and it anchored the new thread as it was spun. Now she took the spindle and held the leader in one hand.

"Gods bless me," she whispered, and dipped into the black contents of the iron bowl. The unmagic was eager to stick to her purified skin. It crawled over her head, seeking an opening. Sandry shuddered.

Taking a deep breath, ordering herself not to think about how bad it felt, she pinched thumb and forefinger together and drew them out of the nothingness. With them came a strand like thin cord. Overlapping it with her cotton leader, Sandry gave both an experienced twist. They wound together. On her next twist, she set the spindle going, letting it whirl around and around. The twist in the joined cotton and unmagic traveled up the dark cord, twirling it, making it stronger and thicker.

In one way the spinning was easy. She never had to worry about the dark cord breaking; one bit of unmagic was always determined to join the rest. She never had to stop as she put darkness to be spun against the end of what she'd already worked, as she did with real fiber. As long as that shadowy pool lay in the iron dish, the nothingness streamed through her hand. Once the dish was empty, she took the finished cord from her spindle, wound it onto a spool, and put the spool in its holder. Then she would empty the next bottle into the dish, remove a strand, and begin to spin again.

That was the easy part.

The unmagic wanted her. It tested her skin and the cracks under her nails. It tried to creep out of her hands and up her chest, seeking her face. She felt as if she wore gloves of it, cool and slimy. As the night wore on she thought, or the nothingness made her think, of letting go, lying back and resting without a thought for tomorrow. It offered no more worries about her uncle, about teaching Pasco, about distant friends. What did people matter, when shadows would have them in the end? it wanted her to think. All she had to do was give in.

She caught herself drifting, and shook off the listlessness that had seeped into her bones. Whipping her magic to a white heat, she sent it coursing through her body, its fire driving the shadows back. She spun harder, winding the darkness so tight that it had nothing left over to pry at her with.

The wind howled. The tent walls flapped, fighting the

magical bonds that held them to the rock platform. Despite the globes that warmed the tent, drafts crept in to make her shiver.

What if it leaked? she wondered in sudden panic. What if this stuff oozed through the rock, bleeding into the ground below? It would spread. The desperate poor of the Mire would give up and starve to death, not caring enough to feed themselves. She could almost see it: babies cried unattended in their cradles; old people called feebly, and no one came to help. Houses burned, no one came to put out the fires. And unmagic crept up to Winding Circle, trickling past the walls, seeping into the water. . . .

Oh, get serious, Duchess! She could hear Briar as clearly as if he stood before her. Is this *real*, or is it just what the goo wants you to think?

What it wants me to think, replied Sandry, and woke up. Her spindle dropped to the floor. While she had sunk into visions of disaster, her spindle had reversed direction, unspinning all she had done with the unmagic from the current bottle. She growled and thrust the dark smears that crawled up her arm back into the iron dish. Taking a few deep breaths, she pulled herself together and began again.

The rain beat down on the tent. The walls brightened somewhat. It was after dawn, but on a day when she could have used some sunshine, it was going to keep raining. Sandry finished another bottle. One more to go.

As she started the last bowlful, the waking dreams began. Duke Vedris was blue-lipped and gray-faced, clutching his left arm as if it pained him. He collapsed in his study, or at the supper table, or fell from his horse. Lark was abed, coughing and coughing, with bright red blood on the handkerchief she held to her lips. Tris burned alive, encased in solid lightning, her skin turning black in the heat. Daja's teacher, Frostpine, turned from an anvil and bashed Daja's head in with his hammer. Vines with thorns as long as a man's hand snaked around Briar and Rosethorn, ripping them to pieces like claws. She smelled blood and rot, dung, urine, and bad things she couldn't name.

She walked into the inner keep, where she had been only twice before. The rooms where they'd put the four Rokat families dripped with blood. Everyone had been chopped to pieces, even the children's pets.

No, thought Sandry fiercely. *No.* She tightened her grip on the nothingness, and used the white heat of her magic to banish it from her mind and heart. *It is going to turn out as I mean it to, without hopelessness or despair, thank you very much!*

Suddenly her clean fingertips met — she was out of darkness. Instantly she grabbed for her spindle as it fell.

A roll of finished unmagic cord wrapped around her spindle's stem. Confused, she looked at the dish. It was empty. No drop of shadow clung to the spelled iron. She checked the bottles. They, too, were empty. She had spun it all.

Sandry wound the cord onto the last spool, and put it away. For the first time since she had dismounted from Russet, she sat. Her feet were swollen and sore; her knees and hands stiff. She let her head fall back for a moment, then looked at that rack of spools. The unmagic on them was tamed, at least for the moment.

Now to fashion her net.

With Alzena's latest wound, everything seemed to go awry. No healer would attend someone they didn't know — they'd all heard about the one who was killed. She and Nurhar should have been able to take the mage's nameless path to the Battle Islands, where healers asked no questions. They should have, but the mage said that after their escape from House Rokat, he could open those paths no longer. It took more strength than he could summon.

Nurhar could have hidden in the mage's spells and kidnapped a healer, but he had been foolish while Alzena was at Duke's Citadel. He had given the mage a dose of dragonsalt. Now the mage could only hum nursery songs. He would be useless until the drug was gone from his body. Alzena wanted to kick Nurhar for his folly, but even the idea of it was tiring.

She suspected that Nurhar wanted to say she had bungled the Citadel exploration, but he, too, seemed not to care. She had made lesser mistakes in their years to-gether and he had screamed at her for them. Now all he wanted to do was huddle by the fire once he had treated her wound.

Alzena joined him there. When meals came, they made themselves eat. They also forced the mage to eat. Left to himself, he would have starved, forgetting everything but the happiness he found in dragonsalt.

He should have asked for more after a day, but he didn't. Three days passed before Alzena figured out why. Somehow the mage had gotten Nurhar's dragonsalt pouch and was dosing himself.

There were Rokats to kill. She still cared about that, so she made herself get moving. She took the drugs from the mage. Then she had a thought: dragonsalt gave strength to those not gifted with magic. She poured a measure of the drug into a cup, mixing it with ale. She drank that down, then fixed another cup for Nurhar. He refused at first, but when she would not let him be, he drank it to silence her. Within half an hour they were changing their filthy clothes, combing out their hair, and cleaning the place up. As they worked, they laid plans. There had to be a way to get at those Rokats.

"Let's try the roof," Nurhar suggested. "Hooks and rope we have in plenty. We go to the palace, get on its roof, then climb to the roof of the inner keep. If it's sep-arate, we swing across on the ropes. We'll go in that way.

I bet they don't have so many guards up above. We can avoid the ones they have. Enough sitting around. Let's move."

"What about him?" Alzena demanded, gesturing at the mage. He was huddled into a ball, furious at losing his dragonsalt, hurting after just an hour without it.

Nurhar opened his medicine pouch and selected a pain ball. He forced it down the mage's throat and held his jaws shut until the mage had swallowed. That would ease the dragonsalt pangs.

"Why can't you just let me die?" he asked bitterly when Nurhar released him. "It's not that far off for me anyway."

"You die when we say," Nurhar snapped. He groped under the bed. "And you go with us," he said, pulling out the carry-frame he'd made after their escape from Rokat House. "If you can't make yourself useful, we'll dump you off the keep. You'll die then, but it'll hurt." He giggled, liking that idea.

Alzena didn't care for a husband who giggled, but she needed to get some Rokats while the dragonsalt made her want to. She helped Nurhar strap the mage to the carry-frame.

The duke had returned to the Citadel by the time Sandry emerged from the tent on Wehen Ridge. On some level of her exhausted mind, the girl was relieved. She knew her uncle might be alarmed if he saw her now, and she hadn't the strength to reassure him.

Do soldiers ever feel like this? she wondered dully as the cart rumbled down Harbor Road to Summersea. Like they've marched and marched until they just want to fall down and die, only to be told they have to keep marching?

She was cold. She was wet from the rain and from the showers that had cleansed her once she finished the net and locked it away. Most of all, she was so tired her bones hurt.

If Tris had been home where she belonged, instead of jauntering to parts unknown, at least Sandry wouldn't be quite so cold and wet. Tris would have sent the storm that continued to buffet Summersea on its way, to make things easier for her friend.

Get some rest, Lark had advised when Sandry got into the cart. Now the girl curled up on the pallet someone had left there, thinking she would never be able to sleep. The thought of sliding across the bed of the cart until she fetched up against the ebony box that held the net gave her the horrors. Looking around, she saw ropes that anchored the canvas cover. They were securely tied, with plenty left over. Sandry called the ends to her wearily. Only when they had wrapped themselves firmly around her waist, holding her away from the box, did she close her eyes.

She woke briefly when the ropes let her go and some-one lifted her out of the cart. She looked around: one of Winding Circle's top mages, Dedicate Crane, was carry-ing her into a cellar. "Where are we?" she mumbled.

"It seems Durshan Rokat has a secret entrance to his home," Crane replied in his usual, energyless murmur. "Now no one will know we're in his house. It's a good thing he volunteered to be bait, is it not? Rest while you can."

She was about to tell him that he was strong for someone so bony. Instead she slept. The next time she woke, she was being gently placed on a divan and cov-ered with a blanket. She muttered and curled up, not wanting to open her eyes a moment before she had to.

She napped until she heard a familiar voice: "Is she going to sleep *forever?*"

Sandry opened her eyes and saw Pasco. "Are we ready?" she asked, yawning as she sat up. The welcome scent of rose-orange tea met her nostrils. With Pasco be-side her, Sandry followed her nose to the kitchen. Lark smiled and pressed a large mug of tea into her hands.

"You left me with the little monster for hours and hours," accused Pasco. "She worked me to death!"

The tea was just cool enough to gulp. Sandry took a large swallow, then replied, "I'm sure the experience was good for you."

"Why do people always say too much work is good?" complained the boy. "I never thought so!"

"But you are lazy to the bone, my lad," replied Lark. "And that's one of my best friends you're calling a 'little monster.'" She gave Sandry two thick pieces of bread with ham and a sliced-up tomato between them. Sandry ate gratefully.

"But she *is* a monster," Pasco argued. "She's trying to kill me." He helped himself to a slice of the iced cake that sat on a counter.

"Can you do that dance *exactly?*" Sandry wanted to know.

Pasco grinned, smug. "Yazmín says if she puts a mark on the floor I can land on it on my toes ten times of ten. She says I have *perfect* body memory."

Sandry glanced at Lark, who winked at her. For someone who called her a monster, Pasco seemed very pleased by Yazmín's praise.

"You have to get it absolutely right," Sandry told Pasco solemnly. "You won't be able to see my net at all."

"I *know*," he said impatiently. "I've only been told a thousand times!"

"Actually, we found a way to cope with that," Lark told Sandry. "Come." She led the girl and Pasco through a doorway as Sandry continued to eat. They entered what had probably been a dining room before the furnishings had all been taken out. Now there were only whitewashed walls, candle sconces, and a tile floor. The entire room — floor, walls, and ceiling — had been thoroughly cleansed by Winding Circle's mages.

Sandry blinked at the floor and began to smile. She doubted that the central pattern of red and white clay tiles — a pattern that matched her net precisely — had been part of the original floor.

"Are you ready to start?" Lark asked her. "It's after one. We fixed the starting time for when the Citadel clock strikes two. That's when Durshan Rokat will leave the inner keep." When they had worked out their plan, the mage council had suggested the Dihanurs would be less suspicious of a trap if they had a reason to come to the net, like following a quarry on his way home.

"He *is* a volunteer?" Sandry wanted to know.

Lark nodded. "His grace talked to Durshan himself. Your uncle insisted on making sure we had a genuine volunteer."

Sandry took a deep breath. "I need something sweet," she told Lark, "another mug of tea, and time to use the privy. After that, I'll be as ready as I can ever be." She had a case of the shakes. Somehow she had the feeling they weren't going to go away — she would just have to work around them.

Lark walked them back to the kitchen. As she cut a slice from the cake, she looked at Pasco. "Go through that door and find the musicians — they're in the front parlor. Tell them we're almost ready. And once your part is done, go home with them. No one will think anything of servants leaving the house."

"Leaving?" cried Pasco. "But I want to see what happens!"

"Absolutely not." Sandry had never heard herself use that tone before, though it sounded like a combination of the duke and Tris. "You are to get away and stay away, understand?" she demanded, holding the boy's eyes with hers. "This isn't a game. I will *not* tell your parents you got killed because I let you stay and watch like this was a performance!"

"For one thing," Lark pointed out, "we don't know they'll even come now. We hope the net will bring them quickly, but if they aren't in this part of the city when Durshan Rokat leaves the Citadel, it may take them a day or two to hear about him."

"Please, Lady Sandry," whined the boy.

Lark took him by the shoulders, turned him around, and thrust him through the door that led to the front hall. "Musicians. Go," she said firmly.

Pasco looked back, hesitated, then obeyed.

As Lark poured a fresh cup of tea and added honey, she asked gravely, "Was it very bad, dear? Spinning the unmagic. Tying the net."

Sandry shivered. "It likes real magic more than anything," she whispered. "It isn't happy if it can't eat what you have, and it never stops trying to get in."

Lark smoothed her hair with a gentle hand. "I would have given anything to spare you that."

Sandry hugged her teacher. "I know."

She finished her cake and her tea, went to the privy, then washed her hands and face in a bucket of water. When she next entered the empty dining room, the musicians stood in the door that led to the front of the house. Pasco waited in a corner. Other council mages came to watch: Crane, Winding Circle's Dedicate Superior, Moonstream, the Duke's healer, Comfrey, and Skyfire, who was the head of the Fire temple, and a handful of others. Sandry knew the plan was that these mages would be outside the house, concealed within spells, standing guard. When Pasco finished the net dance, they would sprinkle the lines of ash across the ways into the house. There was a chance the Dihanurs might leave footprints. If they did, the watchers could give Sandry some warning of the killers' approach.

The Guildhall clock struck two. Up at Duke's Citadel the play they were staging for the Dihanurs was just starting. It was Skyfire, a one-time general, who had devised this part of the plan with the help of the duke and Erdogun. They had no way to know where the assassins were: they might be in the duke's residence, trying to get at the inner keep once more, in the outer bailey of the Citadel, or somewhere between the Citadel and the waterfront. With that in mind, everyone had to act as if their quarry could see them at any moment, from the time Durshan Rokat walked out of the inner keep and demanded to go home. The handful of people who were to create the charade and keep it going had orders to make as much noise and fuss as possible. That way, even if the killers were not watching, they would hear Citadel, Guard, or city gossip about the crazy old man who turned down the duke's hospitality.

Durshan Rokat would be walking out of the inner keep now. It was time for Sandry and Pasco to add the power of their net to the killers' discovery that one Rokat was available to be murdered.

"Have we soldiers to arrest the Dihanurs?" Sandry asked Lark as she opened the ebony box where the net was kept.

"In the cellar and upstairs," Lark replied.

Sandry looked down into the box. Her shadowy creation was invisible against the black wood, but she could feel it there. Tying and knotting the net, she had become attuned to unmagic. It was stronger now, the knots increasing its power as it fed back on itself.

Her skin tingling with fear, she gathered her net in her arms. She had left bits of her own power like yarn ties at the corners so she could find them. Taking the first corner, she placed it on the north point on the pattern, over a round socket in the floor. Lark knelt and fitted an ebony peg into the socket to anchor that corner of the net. Sandry then went to the eastern point of the tile pattern and set another corner of the net there; Crane anchored it with an elderwood peg. South came next; Dedicate Skyfire anchored the unmagic with an oak peg. Last was the west corner; Sandry nodded her thanks to Healer Comfrey, who placed a hawthorn peg to hold the net.

Now Sandry moved back from her creation, trying to ignore the dark film that lay over her clothes. Everything she had worn or used for this working would be burned when this was over. In her vision the dark cords of the unmagic net were stark against the red and white tiles of the floor pattern. Best of all, they matched it perfectly.

"Pasco," she whispered.

As he walked in, Dedicate Skyfire stopped him and pressed a leather pouch into his hand.

"Once you complete the center square," Lark said, pointing, "drop that in the middle, understand?"

Pasco opened the pouch. Moonstream said, "Don't," and Skyfire barked, "Careful with that, boy," as he peeked inside.

Pasco glanced at them, then lowered his nose close to the mouth of the pouch and gave the tiniest of sniffs. When he looked up, he surveyed everyone with eyes that were huge with reproach. "This is dragonsalt."

"That it is," replied Skyfire crisply.

"It's illegal," the boy persisted. "Having it gets you ten years in the granite quarries up north."

Skyfire uttered a bark of laughter. "Nonsense, young Acalon — no one survives ten years in the quarries."

Pasco stared at the tall dedicate, his mouth stubborn. "*Selling* it gets your guts ripped out on Penitence Hill."

Sandry put her hands on her hips. "We know it's bad, Pasco," she said quietly. "It's how their mage has done so much damage without his unmagic eating him alive. It's bait, all right? Otherwise he'll see the net and never step onto it. We'll have the other two and not him."

Pasco nodded and closed the pouch, tucking it into his pocket. He came to stand at the north corner of the net. As the musicians played the opening of the dance tune, Sandry heard him whisper, "Come to me, rats!"

When Pasco heard his cue, he jumped lightly into the center of the first net square. He danced beautifully, his toes flicking one way and another, pointing to each corner. Then he was on to the next square, and the next.

Sandry watched and sweated, terrified he would miss a step and brush the nothingness. Soon she realized there could as well have been yards of space between his feet and those invisible cords for all the closer he came to them. Yazmín had given him movements for his arms and torso that seemed to add to his magic. With each change of position, the silver fire left in his wake grew brighter.

Sandry's other fear, that leaving the dragonsalt pouch in the center square might throw the boy off, was soon banished. She didn't even see him reach for it, but as he jumped to the next square, the pouch slid from his hand. It struck the midpoint of the center square with a soft thump.

Almost before Sandry realized it, Pasco was skipping lightly over the north peg. He stopped, twirled, and bowed deeply to her. The silver fire that had trailed him knotted and sprang back into the pattern of his dance, enclosed on all sides by the unmagic.

"Very good," Skyfire told the boy. "Your part's done now. Scat."

"You heard him," added Moonstream, her face kind. "Very nice work, young Master Acalon. Now go, before your fish swim into this net."

Back inside the duke's residence, Alzena scouted the inner keep again. Perhaps there was a route she had missed, one not so closely watched. She left Nurhar and the mage in a tower room that gave them access to the roof. Then she went to see what she might find, after taking a second dose of dragonsalt. It was amazing stuff. She thought so much better with it in her veins, even if it did make her irritable. Maybe she wouldn't give it up, once she returned home.

What she found was enough to make her start killing everyone she saw, if it hadn't been for her family duty. There were three ways to come at the inner keep — she learned that by listening to servants. When she tried them, she found that entire squads of the Duke's Guard were actually *camped* in the halls — bedrolls, equipment, and even the Guards themselves clumped so closely together that an approach was impossible. No matter how careful she was, the litter of soldiers and possessions guaranteed she would bump into something or someone and rouse the others.

She stood there, hands clenched with fury, glaring at these insects that were ruining her plans. It took a few moments for her to realize that something had stirred the insects up. When their officers were not looking, they were muttering to one another. The subject was the mad old man who had just stalked out of the inner keep, declaring he would go home.

Alzena listened. Could it be? Had a Rokat walked out of his hiding place?

She trotted off through the palace corridors, listening to the talk as she went. When she reached the main hall, she found all the gossip she'd heard was true.

"I have business matters that will not wait!" A richly

dressed man in his sixties was shaking his walking stick at a tall, bald black man whose nostrils curved as if he smelled something bad. The crossed keys badge on his tunic marked him as the duke's seneschal, Erdogun fer Baigh. "If those murdering beasts have not struck by now, it's because they've given up. What do they care for us little fish, anyway?"

"Master Rokat," began the bald man.

"Don't you 'Master Rokat' me, Baron fer Baigh!" cried the older man. "My kinfolk will huddle in that dungeon you call the inner keep if they wish, but Durshan Rokat is going home!" He turned to a cluster of muscled women and men who could only be bodyguards. "I don't pay you to gorge on his grace's food and laze!" he snapped. "We are leaving. Call my chair at once!"

A bodyguard ran to do as he was ordered. Erdogun fer Baigh snapped his fingers for a footman. "Since Master Rokat no longer desires our hospitality," he said, his voice clipped, "tell the watch commander I require two squads of Duke's Guards to accompany him home. Two squads, mind. I want all Summersea to know this man is under the duke's protection." He turned away and began to climb the broad stair that rose from the hall. "You'd think these people didn't *want* to stay alive," he muttered.

Alzena watched the old man and his guards leave,

wondering. They were so close to the inner keep and all those Rokats. But there was that carpet of guards to think of. Perhaps no one here had thought to watch the keep's upper stories as well as the ground floor, but it didn't seem likely. And here was a Rokat — an *old* one, as old as Palaq Dihanur had been when Rokats cut off his head — who insisted that he return to his house.

Every instinct clamored for her to go after the old man. Her Dihanur masters had taught her that as one of her first lessons: take the weak and easy prey first. No matter that his was one of the houses they hadn't scouted before they killed Jamar Rokat — tracking Durshan would be as easy as breathing, with all those guards around him. People would talk of their passing for hours: the Dihanurs need only follow the gossip.

Take the weak, easy, and stupid prey first. Those families in the inner keep were going nowhere, and finding that carpet of guards had discouraged her. A killing today would improve her mood. Letting this prey escape was mad. What if he reached his house, stayed a few hours or a day, lost his courage, and returned? She wouldn't even have his head to display somewhere — somewhere like this large, drafty entrance hall. Maybe the sight of a fresh head would give this cursed Duke Vedris another heart attack. In the confusion of his collapse, who was to say they wouldn't relax their guard on the inner keep?

This sense of rightness was the most powerful feeling she'd had in a long time. She knew it in her gut: Durshan Rokat's killing would break this cycle of frustration.

When she reached the room where she had left her husband and the mage, she found Nurhar wild with energy and the mage shivering. Quickly she told them about the old man and the human carpet. "He's a spoiled elder with no more brains than a rabbit," she told Nurhar. "I want his head."

Nurhar caught fire over the idea, too. He hoisted the mage into his carry-frame. "Cover us well," he told their charge as he tightened the straps. "No slip-ups."

"I never slip up," mumbled the mage. "I'm not the one who got cut and needed a healer you had to ki —"

Alzena slapped his face. "If you are not silent, I will cut out your tongue," she whispered.

He stared at her with eyes that were set in deep black circles, with no trace of white remaining. "How're you different from the pirates?" he wanted to know. "They hit me when they felt grumpy, too."

Nurhar crouched beside him. "She didn't mean it," he told the mage. "She's just frustrated. We're all frustrated."

The mage hid his face in his hands. "There is something about this place," he whispered through his fingers. "All these spells. Centuries of them. Centuries . . . Take me out of here. Closer to Durshan Rokat's house, perhaps I can do something. Yes." He looked at them, black eyes glistening. "Yes, get me closer. The air here is bad for me — too many spells. Once in the city I can work better."

"You'd better find a way to handle all the spells here," Nurhar said, his voice ice. "Once we've got the old man, we're coming back." He picked up the mage's carry-frame and slung it on his back. "You'll get us into that inner keep if I have to use your head as a battering ram."

Pasco was following the musicians out when he rebelled. This wasn't right. He wanted to see his net work. They were treating him like a child, when they might have no chance to get these rats without him. He was going to stay, that was all there was to it.

But how? In a moment those mages would come out of the net room. They would disappear within spells to make them look like part of the house, or the garden, or the street outside. He'd heard them talk about that. If they saw him, they would make him go.

Suddenly he remembered something from the day before. Yazmín had been teaching allurement dances. One had a movement that caught his imagination: the dancer held an arm straight out with the hand at right angles to the arm. The dancer then pulled the other hand over her face with the fore and middle fingers parted in a sideways arrow. While one hand traveled across the eyes, the dancer looked sidelong at the outstretched hand. Yazmín had called it a "flirt." Pasco thought it also looked like something that — with a bit of magic behind it — might achieve the opposite result. It could make people look *away* from the person who made it. Their eyes might slide off the mage; they might never see him.

Standing in the hall, he closed his eyes and took his seven-count breaths, holding them and letting them go as he'd been taught. The feeling he was beginning to know was his magic, a kind of fizzy tingle, filled him almost instantly. He gracefully lifted his left arm, holding it out palm up and outward, as he let his power roll down it. Now he raised his right hand, forming the arrow with forefinger and middle finger. He drew it across his eyes as he looked sidelong at his left hand. While he did these things, he cast some of that fizzy sense out through his left arm, and poured more through his right hand, making it flow away from him.

The woman they called Moonstream emerged from the dining room, talking to redheaded Skyfire. "I hope this works," she said. "Otherwise we may have to do something drastic."

Skyfire bark-laughed. "Any ideas on what this drastic thing will be?"

Moonstream shook her head. "Not a one," she said ruefully. They walked right by Pasco. "How often are we called on to deal with a mage like this, anyway?"

They didn't see me! I did it! Pasco thought gleefully, struggling to hang on to his power. I worked a magic all by myself!

Now for a place to hide. The corner of the kitchen between the hearth and the cupboards seemed best. No one would stand guard in that part of the house at all, in case the rats came in that way, and Pasco could hear everything that went on in the dining room from there. Just now Dedicate Lark was telling Lady Sandry, "I'll be downstairs with the guards. Call if you need help."

"Of course," Lady Sandry assured her. "Pasco did a good job, didn't he?"

Pasco beamed.

"The boy has talent," Lark said. "Don't forget to conceal yourself, my darling. You don't want them to see you until they've stepped into the net."

"I'll be fine," Lady Sandry assured her.

Dedicate Lark walked in from the dining room. For a moment she hesitated, frowning. Pasco felt the tiniest, most delicate shift under him, as if someone were tugging a rug from under his feet. Hurriedly he called up his power again, and drew his hand over his eyes once more. Look away, look away, he thought.

At last Dedicate Lark shrugged, and went to the cellar door. She stopped, checked around one last time, then went downstairs.

Alzena, Nurhar, and the mage caught up with Durshan Rokat just past the Arsenal gates, in a snarl of people and horses caused by an overturned wagon on Spicer Street. Once they would have been amused by the Guards' frustration over the delay and their fear that the Dihanurs might try to kill the old man there. Alzena thought they could have spared themselves that worry. Seeing all those people in the halls to the inner keep had made her jumpy. There were too many chances here to collide with someone and be caught. Instead they watched the old man and his protectors dully, waiting until the tangle cleared.

When it did, they kept well back from Rokat, but followed him all the way home. They went a scant block away when he entered the gateyard of his house, leaving the Duke's Guards to position themselves on the street side of his property wall. None of them looked happy;

they heard one woman tell her lieutenant, "May as well draw a target on his head, the old fool."

Half of the hired bodyguards went into the house ahead of Rokat to make sure no one lay in wait. When they signaled, Durshan trotted inside. The rest of his bodyguard sat around the gateyard. From the looks on their faces, they were not happy with the situation. They grumbled to one another, sharpened weapons, and kept an eye on the gate.

Alzena disliked the thought of passing among them on her way to the front door as much as she had disliked making an attempt on Spicer Street. She and Nurhar conferred in the softest of whispers, still a block away from their target's house. They knew that the chances were the back door and roof were watched, since the guards would know how Alzena had entered Fariji Rokat's house. It was Nurhar who remembered they still carried the hooks and ropes meant for use at Duke's Citadel. Within minutes they had stolen into a garden belonging to Durshan Rokat's neighbor, and climbed over the high wall into the old man's garden.

Alzena and Nurhar were giddy: after days of frustration and dead ends, they were close to a kill. Even the mage seemed to catch the fever. He softly urged them to hurry inside.

Pantry and kitchen alike were empty. They hesitated, wondering where the old man might have gone. Then

Alzena distinctly heard his voice in the next room. She started for it, but stopped when she felt Nurhar's hand on her arm. She couldn't have seen it if he had pointed, so he turned her chin until she saw the corner beside the hearth. A slice of cake hung in midair. Crumbs dripped from it as an invisible mouth took a bite.

Alzena lunged for the cake and pressed a body into the corner. She guessed where that mouth was and covered it with one hand. Magic evaporated. A wide-eyed boy appeared. He scrabbled at her with clutching hands, able to feel her if not see her.

She felt Nurhar against her back and heard his softest whisper: "Cover him, mage."

There was a creak of the carry-frame and a ghostly spell-whisper. The boy vanished, this time cloaked in unmagic. Alzena gripped his waist with one arm, using her free hand to keep his mouth covered.

He fought her madly now. Of course, she thought. He doesn't even have an eye slit to show him the real world is still here. For all his struggles, she easily kept him under control as she maneuvered him through the door into the next room.

It was empty, as bare as if no one lived here. No, that wasn't true. A pouch lay at the center of the tiled floor.

Hidden by woven air that made her seem like part of the wall, Sandry was absently unweaving and reweaving a part of her skirt when something thumped in the kitchen. It wasn't Durshan Rokat. He was upstairs, ringed by guards; he had obeyed orders and gone straight to his protectors. Sandry was the only one on the ground floor of the house.

She sat up, all her senses alert. None of the sentry mages had warned her, but the chance that they would detect the killers' approach had always been small.

Come on, she thought, not daring to twitch, hoping it was them and not a mouse. You feel the net calling you. If it does what I think, you'll believe what you want most is right in here. . . .

Dark-smeared air rolled into the dining room from the kitchen and passed over her spell-net. From its position on the floor the net began to ripple and rise, shaping itself around solid forms.

She heard feet scuffle, then a grunt. Wood creaked; cloth rustled. A chunk of shadow separated from the main body of it and fell hard, as a body falls, beside the pouch of dragonsalt at the heart of the net. There was a snarl from the larger darkness. The pouch rose in the air, opened, turned over to spill out a mound of the drug, then straightened. The mound disappeared, as if someone unseen had popped it into his mouth.

"Alzena, I'm caught!" whispered a man's voice. "I can't pull free!"

"Curse you for a useless piece of mule dung, mage," a hoarse female voice said. "Take the spells off *now*."

Sandry felt a touch of panic before she remembered that she was hidden from view. The woman was talking to someone else.

"I don't want to," a high, trembling voice said from the unmagic near the dragonsalt pouch. "I like the spells. I like it *here*."

The shadow patterns of the spell-net rippled while the unseen people talked. Its cords draped and twined around the larger mass, then sent out a number of tendrils. Each turned into a small fan at the tip. Not fans, she realized as dark hair on two heads slowly appeared at the top of the tallest shadow. My net isn't spreading out; it's sucking the unmagic *in*.

She was beginning to see one forehead when the female voice said, "Take the unmagic off us or I'll cut you up, you ungrateful ratbirth."

"Suit yourself," replied the high voice, now a little slurred.

Four people appeared at the heart of the net. One, hidden by two standing adults, was struggling wildly. Of the two who kept still, one was a man, brown-haired, brown-eyed, dressed in the plain breeches, shirt, and boots worn by many commoners. Sandry recognized him vaguely from the fight in Jamar Rokat's countinghouse.

On his back was a frame like those that woodcutters used to carry their wares. Empty straps dangled from it. He bent over a smaller person on the floor — their mage, thought Sandry uneasily — grabbed him by the arm, and pulled him upright.

Looking at the mage, Sandry realized why she had thought he was sunk into a pool of unmagic that day at Rokat House. He had no legs. His coarse breeches were folded and pinned around stumps that ended at mid-thigh. He clutched the dragonsalt pouch tightly with both hands. He was dark-haired and sallow, terribly thin.

He's Pasco's age, thought Sandry in horror. She hadn't realized that at their first meeting.

"Show yourself," growled the other standing adult. "I know there are mages here." It was a woman, big-hipped, black-haired, dressed in the same anonymous clothing as the man. Her back was to Sandry. Now she turned, revealing the fourth member of the group. "Too bad your kitchen sentry couldn't keep his hands off the cake."

She held Pasco easily. She had wrapped an arm around his neck, the crook of her elbow under his chin. Now she yanked, pulling the back of Pasco's head against her shoulder. Her free hand held a dagger to the boy's unprotected throat. There was a wild look in her black eyes; her grin bared all of her yellowing teeth. She looked like a furious mule.

"Oh, Pasco," whispered Sandry. She picked up the

spindle that she'd been keeping on her lap and stood, shedding the magical veil that had made her corner of the room seem empty.

"You?" the man asked scornfully. "You're barely more than a child yourself! What have you to do with this?"

He and the woman struggled to yank free of the net's clinging strands, without success. It held them in place as firmly as if they were glued there.

Sandry knew better than to tell them Pasco was her student. That would simply give them more power over her than they already had. "Did these people cut off your legs?" she asked the boy on the floor, keeping her voice gentle.

He looked up at her, and Sandry took a step back. There were not whites to his eyes, no pupils or irises — just nothingness. Unmagic riddled his entire body. Very few spots left were untainted. He was draining into the cords of her net.

"Pirates done my legs," he said lazily, his voice slurred with dragonsalt. "Alzena 'n Nurhar're my frien's. They give me this." He hoisted the drug pouch and frowned. "But they keep takin' it away. They want my magic like the pirates done."

"I'll bet they do," whispered Sandry. She turned her eyes on the adults — Alzena and Nurhar, the boy mage had called them. "Surrender," she told them.

"I think not," Alzena said, drawing the knife-point

down Pasco's neck. A thin line of blood followed it as Pasco whimpered. "I can make this killing last." She shifted her grip on Pasco to hold him more firmly still. "This net here is your doing? You let us go, and he'll live."

Sandry watched Alzena and Nurhar. Both were striped with unmagic. They had worn the spells too long without being cleansed, if they had even known cleansing was necessary. Before long the shadow would devour them as it had this boy.

If she let them go to save Pasco, who else might they kill before they stopped existing? Would they even keep their word not to kill him? They had to like what they did, surely, to do so much of it.

Her palms were damp. "I beg you, let him go. He's nothing to you."

"Sure enough," replied Alzena with that teeth-baring grin. "But he's something to you, isn't he? Free us." Again the dagger trailed down Pasco's throat, leaving a second cut to ooze blood. Pasco screamed and thrashed against her imprisoning arm. The cry was strangled; she had jerked against his chin, closing his mouth.

"We don't want the guards to hear our little talk. And they're about, aren't they?" Alzena wanted to know. "Not in earshot, or they'd hear us now, but upstairs, maybe? Downstairs? Free us. We'll loose the boy once we're out the gate, and run like lightning."

Coldness settled in Sandry's mind. Everything was very still and clear. Will you really? she thought, weighing their deeds against Alzena's words. Or will you just keep taking hostages until someone puts an arrow through you? How many will you slaughter before an archer gets a killing shot?

Pasco's eyes met hers, pleading. Blood trickled in two streams down his neck. He was her student. She should have known he would try to stay behind and watch.

"I have to take up the pegs at the corners," Sandry replied. She didn't have to pretend to be frightened; her fear was close enough to grasp and use. "Once that's done, I can roll up the net. Just — please, don't hurt Pasco. Please don't." If she pleaded, she knew, they would think her weak.

"Don't beg, wench," Alzena told her. "It just makes me angry. Get your pox-rotted pegs." The dagger flicked along the line of Pasco's jaw, opening a third cut.

That chilled Sandry to the bone. She went clockwise around the edges of the net, removing the pegs from their sockets with her free hand. The other hand, the one on the side turned away from the captives, held her spindle.

"This net's pretty," the boy mage remarked when she was at the south peg. "I never tried making things with unmagic. No one ever taught me."

"Little is known about your magic," Sandry replied, nearing the last — the north — peg.

There was a muffled squeal from Pasco. This time Alzena had cut straight across his chest, and not a thin scratch. "Don't talk!" she ordered. "Just free us!"

Passing the door to the front hall and the window, Sandry discovered they were not alone. The guards upstairs and someone downstairs must have heard voices talking. People were looking into the dining room, trying to think of ways to stop this. She knew they were asking themselves if they could take the Dihanurs before they hurt Pasco any more, and she knew they could not. Alzena was too fast with her knife.

Putting the north peg aside, Sandry looked at her student. *All he wants is to dance and have fun,* she thought.

Days ago — was it only days? — she had taken a strand of his magic from him and kept it inside her, so she could always find him at need. Now she grasped that thread and sent a rush of her own magic through it, making it rope-strong.

"Just one more thing, and you'll be free," she told her captives. "I have to unspin the magic that's in my net, otherwise it will keep hold of you." Picking up the edge of the net, she broke the cord and tacked one end of it to the leader on her spindle.

"No tricks," Alzena growled, her voice barely human. "I would be so happy to gut this boy of yours."

"No tricks," agreed Sandry meekly. "I just have to gather the net on the spindle to make it release you. You've seen how they work." Thrusting her power into the spindle, she gave it a quick, hard twirl. It whirled faster than she could hold; she dropped it from a hand that blistered immediately. The knots in the unmagic were falling apart, the force of the spindle twining the net into a single thick rope. It would also spin every single drop of unmagic that was touching the net.

Sandry watched Alzena. She saw the woman's eyes widen when she felt the first gentle tug. Before the woman knew she'd been tricked, Sandry yanked hard on the rope that bound her to Pasco. It pulled him out of Alzena's grip and threw him into the wall. He staggered to his feet, his cuts bleeding.

The boy mage felt it first. He began to giggle, spreading his arms as the spindle drew on all the nothingness in him, pulling him into the net and winding him up like thread.

Now Alzena and Nurhar realized they were in trouble. Their still-living flesh, unlike the mage's, was only veined with nothingness. What was left of their real bodies was being pulled apart. The spindle whirled, its tip smoking against the tiled floor. Now the Dihanurs were dragged across the room, their flesh battling the magic's pull. It bulged between the strands of darkness that were being drawn from them; the unmagic cut into them like silk threads as it twined onto the spindle.

Sandry held Alzena's eyes with hers. She could see when the woman knew what must happen if this were not stopped.

"Please . . ." It was Nurhar who asked, not Alzena.

Sandry shook her head.

Their bodies exploded in a crimson shower, sending pieces everywhere. The impact slammed Pasco into the wall a second time, covering him and Sandry with blood. He slumped to the floor and vomited helplessly.

EPILOGUE

"I'm still not sure I approve of moving in with dancers," Gran'ther Edoar said. He watched as Pasco loaded a seabag full of clothes into the cart that would carry him to Yazmín's school. "If your net-dancing can be used to trap rats, and you can direct where and when people look at you, it seems you are better suited to harrier work than we guessed. What can you learn of that from this female?"

"This is better, Gran'ther." Though it gave him quivers to argue with the old man, Pasco forced himself to say it. "If I only put my magic to harrying, well —" He hesitated, trying to put into words what he had learned in Durshan Rokat's dining room. "If I don't understand my magic, the good and the bad, I'm not a mage at all. I'm just a tool, to be used, like that poor chuff' the killers were using. Anyone could put their hand to me, and make me work however they want, if they figure out how to control me. That's not counting the trouble I might get myself into, not knowing what I can do and what I can't."

"Well, at least you've learned that much," commented Halmaedy. She had come to see Pasco's departure along with Gran'ther and Pasco's mother.

Pasco sneered at his oldest sister. To his grandfather and the silent Zahra he said, "Lady Sandry will keep me out of trouble whilst I learn. And the little monster'll work me so hard I won't have the strength to get into mischief."

"If we can go?" asked the carter, her voice a little too patient, "It's comin' on to rain, and I got bundles to deliver, too."

Zahra kissed her son's forehead. "We'll expect you to supper every Firesday," she told Pasco sternly. "Come say hello if things bring you to East District."

"Mama, it's not like I'm leaving the city!" cried Pasco, laughing. "I'm just going to Festival Street!"

"Mind your teachers!" Gran'ther told him as he climbed up beside the carter. "We don't want to hear of you giving any trouble!"

Pasco grinned and waved as the cart started forward. He knew very well that between Yazmín and Lady Sandry, *he* was the one in for trouble.

Sandry halted on the doorstep at Discipline cottage. A pudgy young man in a novice's white habit sat at the table, awkwardly fitting together the pieces of a table loom. He stared at her, jaw hanging open.

She wasn't quite sure what to say. "Is — is Lark —"

The young man lurched to his feet and ran to the back of the house. He scrambled up the narrow stair to the garret.

"Comas, what on earth —" Lark came out of her workshop, a bolt of cloth in her hands. She noticed Sandry in the doorway. "Well! Look at you!" She put the cloth on the table and came to Sandry, hands out-stretched. "You had people worried!"

Sandry nodded, hugging her teacher. For days after that dreadful meeting with the Dihanurs and their mage, she had kept to her rooms at Duke's Citadel, eating lit-tle, thinking a great deal. She'd had to force herself to talk to Pasco a week later. Even then she had done it only because the duke had said the boy thought she was furi-ous with him because he'd been caught.

Once she had reassured Pasco, it seemed that life would not let her alone. There was Yazmín, who wanted to talk about his training. Lark visited to say that she had been watching Pasco's lessons at Yazmín's, but it looked as if the novice weaver she'd mentioned on Sandry's last visit was indeed a mage. Moreover, he was too shy to deal with more than one or two people at a time. She really needed to concentrate on him, at Discipline. Erdogun had a tantrum with the Residence housekeeper in

Sandry's hearing: he told the woman that he'd gotten very fond of having Lady Sandrilene cover these matters; had servants no minds of their own to use?

The duke came for advice on matters of taste. What colors were flattering to him, what gifts might please a woman of experience and which were too overpowering, did he look older or younger when he rode in a carriage? That had actually been the first light moment in Sandry's release from self-hate: the discovery that her hopes for the duke and Yazmín had borne fruit.

The final spur to her return to the larger world came as three letters in two days, one from Briar, one from Daja, and one from Tris. All were thick; all wanted to know why she hadn't written. They were full of news about what they did and what they had seen. They brimmed with life. They made her present world look shadowy by comparison, and shadows, Sandry realized at last, were the one thing she did not want in her mind.

"I've been very silly," she told Lark now.

"You did a very hard thing, for reasons that everyone agreed were right," Lark said firmly. "You acted as an adult, and you did it without hate. I'm not sure I could have done it without hating them, after seeing that poor maimed boy."

"There's blood on my hands," whispered Sandry, looking at them.

"Good. As long as you feel that way, you won't become like them, will you?" asked Lark.

Sandry shook her head. "You never did have sympathy for the glooms. Maybe I should have come back here afterward."

Lark put the teakettle on. "Should you?" she asked. "It seems to me it would have been like putting off your fine gowns and donning the dresses you wore when you were six."

It was Sandry's turn to gape, slack jawed, like the boy who had run upstairs. "You think so?"

Lark laughed. "My dear, you've moved into the greater world, whether you wished to or not," she said. "As a teacher, as a noble. You've outgrown Discipline. You're getting ready to take your place on the adult stage. Pasco was just the beginning."

Sandry propped her elbows on the table and rested her chin on her hands. "Remember that day you brought Yazmín to the residence? You knew then I was going to live there permanently, didn't you? You didn't seem at all surprised when Uncle said he wanted to start entertaining at this winter with me for hostess."

Lark got down three cups, including Sandry's, and put out honey and a loaf of spice bread. Sandry began to cut up the loaf. "I knew how close you two had become since you went there," the woman replied. "You would miss each other terribly, if you moved back here, and he might well return to bad habits. And you're learning a great deal from him, all of it good. Comas," she called, "if you don't come down, Sandry and I will eat all the spice bread ourselves."

"He's the new student?" asked Sandry. "He's a bit odd."

"He isn't odd." Lark put three plates on the table. "He's so shy it half-cripples him, poor thing. He agrees with nearly anything he's told to do, which is how he became a novice in the first place. I've got my work cut out for me, to break him of *that*."

"You'll find a way," Sandry told her. "You always do."

Lark cupped Sandry's face in her hands. "You and I are not finished, my heart's own. There is still much we can learn from each other, and you're the closest thing to a daughter I will ever have."

Sandry hugged Lark fiercely. "Then I can come back, if I don't like living at the Citadel?"

"Whenever you want," Lark said firmly. "You can even have your old room."

Sandry released her and gazed at the stairs. It had given her a pang, to know a stranger was in the rooms she and her friends had shared, but it looked as if this Comas needed Discipline as much as any of them ever had.

And she knew Lark. If Lark said they were not finished with each other, that Sandry was as good as her own blood, then perhaps Sandry could afford to be generous.

"Let him have my room," she heard herself tell Lark. "That way he doesn't have to run so far to hide."

Lark rested a hand on Sandry's shoulder. "You needn't do that. You know Daja sleeps mostly at the forge when she's here at Winding Circle."

Sandry nodded. "My room's got better light for a weaver," she replied quietly. "And it's nice, being next to your workshop. I used to listen to you weave, late at night. I bet Comas would like that, too."

"Then why don't you go and tell him yourself?" asked Lark. "He knows you are my student — you can reassure him that you aren't jealous."

Sandry got to her feet. "I have an idea," she said. "My student is too outgoing, and yours isn't outgoing enough. We'll mash them together and teach them as one boy. Then we'll mix them up a little and make two new boys who are almost perfect. Teachers will come from everywhere to guess our secret."

"Mila, don't let Comas hear you," said Lark, her eyes dancing. "He might think we could actually do it."

Sandry grinned. She walked back to the stairs, and began to climb. There are other mage kids out there, she thought. Some get lucky and get found, like Pasco, or they get shipped to where they could get found, like this Comas. But the pirates found that poor boy, and then the Dihanurs, and they used him up.

I must keep in mind to watch for other mage kids. And I'll write Tris, and Briar, and Daja, and tell them. We were lucky. It's time we spread our luck to others, I think.

ABOUT THE AUTHOR

Tamora Pierce is a full-time writer whose fantasy books include *The Circle of Magic*, *The Song of the Lioness*, *The Immortals* quartets, and *First Test*. She says of her beginnings as an author that "after discovering fantasy and science fiction in the seventh grade, I was hooked on writing. I tried to write the same kind of stories I read, except with teenaged girl heroes — not too many of those around in the 1960s."

In her *Circle of Magic* quartet, Ms. Pierce introduced the four unforgettable mages-in-training who are now four years older in *The Circle Opens* – Sandry, Briar, Daja, and Tris. She began the new quartet at the urging of her many readers, who encouraged her through letters and e-mails to explore the mages' lives further. She chose their next turning point to be when they each acquire their first students in magecraft.

Ms. Pierce lives in New York City with her husband, their three cats (Scrap, Vinnie, and Ferret), two parakeets (Zorak and the Junior Birdman), and "a floating population of rescued wildlife, from mice to crows and chickens." Her Web site address is http://www.sff.net/people/Tamora.Pierce.

Other Books by Tamora Pierce

The Circle of Magic Quartet

Sandry's Book

Tris's Book

Daja's Book

Briar's Book

The Song of the Lioness Quartet

Alanna

In the Hands of the Goddess

The Woman Who Rides Like a Man

Lioness Rampant

The Immortals Quartet

Wild Magic

Wolf-Speaker

Emperor Mage

The Realms of the Gods

F
Pie
mag

Pierce, Tamora.

Magic steps.

$16.95   33415   101356

000799   1121236